D1499745

A GIRL LIKE JANET

**Center Point
Large Print**

Also by Debbie Macomber and available from Center Point Large Print:

Hannah's List
Turn in the Road
Same Time, Next Year
Mail-Order Bride
Return to Promise

**This Large Print Book carries the
Seal of Approval of N.A.V.H.**

A GIRL LIKE JANET

Debbie Macomber

CENTER POINT PUBLISHING
THORNDIKE, MAINE

This Center Point Large Print edition
is published in the year 2012 by arrangement with
Debbie Macomber, Inc.

The text of this Large Print edition is unabridged.
In other aspects, this book may vary
from the original edition.
Printed in the United States of America
on permanent paper.
Set in 16-point Times New Roman type.

ISBN: 978-1-61173-268-9

Library of Congress Cataloging-in-Publication Data

Macomber, Debbie.
A girl like Janet / Debbie Macomber. — Large print ed.
p. cm. — (Center Point large print edition)
ISBN 978-1-61173-268-9 (library binding : alk. paper)
1. Large type books. I. Title.
PS3563.A2364G57 2012
813'.54—dc23

2011044913

Spring 2012

Dear Friends,

I still remember the first time I sat down at a computer. All those buttons, such as F1, F2, PrtScn and ScrLk, terrified me. (Come to think of it, they still do!) Thankfully I had someone with me who willingly calmed my fears. Still, all I really wanted to know was how to type my chapter, store the chapter and print the chapter. Oh, how times have changed from the days when I first rented a typewriter and set it up at our kitchen table.

I wrote A GIRL LIKE JANET shortly after acquiring my first computer, an Eagle, as I remember. The plot revolves around Janet, who is faced with the challenging task of switching from her trusty Selectric typewriter to a computer. Generally, when my books are reissued, I do my best to update the terminology and work in as much modern technology as possible. Attitudes have drastically changed over the years as well. I find it jarring when the problem could be quickly resolved with a cell phone, but back in the 1980s there simply was no such thing. Unfortunately, with A GIRL LIKE JANET, making these changes is impossible. The plot is too specific to the 1980s and Janet's challenge.

So, my friends, this is VINTAGE Debbie Macomber, written long before there was Internet access, e-mail, cell phones, iPods, and other modern conveniences. Still, as I read it, I enjoyed the story and I hope you will, too.

With warmest regards,

Debbie Macomber

To my grandson James Buckley—
a dedication just for him!

Chapter One

"Janet, can I see you in my office a minute." The low-pitched male voice boomed irritably through the intercom.

As a matter of course Janet reached for a steno pad and pencil. The chair rolled back as she stood. Outside the connecting door she paused to push up her glasses from the tip of her nose and replace a stray strand of chestnut-colored hair in the carefully coiled chignon.

Reese Edwards glanced up from the cluttered, disorganized desk when she entered the room. "Sit down," he ordered curtly.

Unconsciously Janet released a soft sigh as she sat. How anyone could work from a desk buried in financial reports, cost sheets, files and correspondence she didn't know.

At the sound of her released breath, Reese glanced up and frowned. "Is there something wrong, Miss Montgomery?"

"No," she denied with a shake of her head, her back straightening. "Of course not."

Janet sat quietly as she watched him continue scribbling almost indecipherable notes across the top of two reports. Dark hair fell forward across the creased lines of his brow. He was handsome, but not in the normal sense. It was the force of his personality that was boldly defined in the proud line of his jaw and the set of his mouth. He was capable of making a clearer statement with one quirk of his brow than some men say in a ten-page brief. Watching him now, Janet realized something was troubling him. After two years of working with Reese she was well acquainted with his moods. Almost from the moment he walked in the door this morning, she had been aware of the restrained anger.

"Have these back to me this afternoon." He stood, uncoiling his six-foot frame from the chair, and handed her the reports. "And, Janet—" He paused; a nerve jerked in the hard line of his jaw. "Phone the jeweler and order a bracelet for Barbara Martin."

Already? her mind questioned. Reese hadn't been seeing Barbara Martin for more than a month. His women usually lasted at least three. So that was what was wrong. "Is there anything else?" she asked as she stood.

"Yes," he said without emotion and escorted her to the door. "Send the standard message with the bracelet."

"Yes, I will." The door clicked softly as it closed. Reaching for the phone to call the jeweler, Janet estimated it would take less than a week to meet Barbara Martin.

She was right; she met the petite blonde two days later. The powder blue eyes were red and puffy when she walked into the office.

"Would it be possible to see Mr. Edwards?" she asked, her soft voice quivering.

Another blonde. Janet would have staked her paycheck on the fact. All Reese's women were blue-eyed blondes. Fragile, thin creatures that were clones of the ones who had preceded them and the ones that would follow. If anything, Reese Edwards was consistent.

"I'm sorry"—Janet's voice was soft with apology—"but Mr. Edwards is in a meeting." She hated to put Miss Martin off. The one thing she detested about her job was having to deal with her boss's women.

Tears welled in the other woman's eyes, and she bit into her trembling bottom lip. "You're supposed to say that, aren't you?" Barbara Martin sobbed, her voice high-pitched and emotional.

Janet took several tissues from her bottom drawer and handed them to the blonde. It was amazing that a city the size of Denver contained so many women exactly alike.

"You can tell Reese that I won't stand for it; he can't do this to me." She paused to blow her nose.

The long tirade, which Janet had heard several times before, continued. The words were different but the message was the same.

Sobbing and near hysterical by the time she'd finished, Barbara slumped into the leather couch. "I love him so much," she wailed. "How . . . how can he do this to me?"

"I don't know," Janet said in soothing tones. "Here, drink this. You'll feel better."

Barbara accepted the Styrofoam cup of coffee and sniffled. "I'm sorry, I didn't mean to burden you with my problems."

"You haven't," Janet assured her. She sat and talked with the blonde until Barbara had composed herself. Twenty minutes later the woman left.

No sooner had Janet returned from escorting her to her red sports car than Reese stepped into the outer office.

"There's nothing I hate worse than a crying female."

Janet's blue eyes widened at the irony of it all. Reese didn't mind breaking their hearts, but he hated to see them cry. It took great restraint on her part not to make some caustic remark.

Reese's flickering gaze touched her. "Don't look so put out," he said in cutting tones. "It's not part of your job."

"Neither is dealing with your female companions," she shot back in a rare display of anger.

"Claws, Janet? You surprise me."

Jerking open the bottom desk drawer, she removed her purse. "If you'll excuse me, I'm already late for lunch."

"Take an extra half hour," he told her.

"Don't worry, I will."

Gail Templeton was waiting for her in the small cafe where they met for lunch and smiled as Janet joined her.

"Whew, you look fit to be tied. What's wrong?"

Janet pulled out the chair and sat down, automatically reaching for the menu.

"Nothing that tarring and feathering Reese Edwards wouldn't fix," she said without elaborating.

Gail looked up from the menu. "Is the great white hunter up to his old tricks again?"

Janet expelled her breath in an uneven sigh. "You don't know the half of it."

"Want to talk about it?" Gail asked in a gentle voice.

Janet smiled her appreciation. "Not now." Gail was probably the best roommate she could ever find. The two girls had met at work right after Janet had been hired as the secretary to the vice president, Malcolm Hayes. Janet was still living with her parents while Gail was struggling to make ends meet in a tiny studio apartment. By pooling their resources they were able to move into an attractive place and establish their independence.

Although she lived with Gail, Janet kept in close contact with her family. Her father was the pastor of a small nondenominational church not far from her apartment. Janet not only attended but was an active, involved member of the congregation. Besides singing in the choir, she taught fifth-grade boy and girl Cadets for the Wednesday night program. Gail also attended the same church.

"How did your morning go?" Janet asked, steering the subject away from her boss.

"All right." She shrugged her shoulders noncommittally. "What can you expect for a Thursday." Her eyes focused on the menu again.

"Thursday, what's wrong with Thursday?"

Gail laughed. "Nothing Friday won't cure."

By the time Janet returned to her desk she realized she was going to have to rush and finish the cost overrun report if she was going to have it ready before leaving that afternoon.

The phone rang repeatedly. Reese was attending an outside meeting and there was a stack of messages waiting for him when he sauntered into the office with Malcolm Hayes an hour later.

"Is that report ready yet?" he questioned as he sorted through the pink slips of paper listing who had called and for what purpose.

"Not yet," Janet said tight-lipped, hiding her irritation as she realized she'd just typed the same paragraph twice.

"Do I detect a note of impatience, Miss Montgomery?" he teased. "You do realize how much more effectively your time could be spent if you had a word processor, don't you?"

The keys of the typewriter blurred as she repressed the panicky sensation. "I prefer my typewriter," she said in an even, monotone voice that, she prayed, wouldn't reveal her dismay.

"Reese, let's go over those figures again."

Janet could have kissed Malcolm Hayes. Reese had mentioned changing over to a word processor several times. So far Janet had been able to fend off the suggestion. But more and more offices were making the switch and she knew the time was coming when she would be faced with the inevitable.

She didn't finish the report until after six. Three times she was forced to retype a page that consisted of columns of figures. Reese had gone down to a warehouse and she promised to have the report on his desk before leaving. Normally such an involved paper wouldn't have caused her problems, but she was still upset from her encounter with Barbara Martin that morning. At least that's what she told herself. Or perhaps it was knowing that sooner or later she would be facing the mechanics of working a computer.

The metro bus dropped her off a block from her apartment building. The aroma of simmering beef gently assaulted her as she opened the door and she paused to inhale the tantalizing smell.

"You're late." Gail stuck her head around the kitchen door and the auburn-colored hair fell over her shoulder.

"I had that report to finish," Janet explained, kicking off her pumps and flexing her toes in the plush living room carpet.

"Are you eating at home tonight or are you and Joel going out?"

Joel was Janet's thirteen-year-old brother. He had been born when Janet was nine. Despite his mental challenges, he was a special child in many ways. Trusting, gentle and happy, Joel brought joy into the lives he touched. Thursday nights were reserved for Janet's younger brother.

"I thought I'd take him bowling tonight. Joel's never been and I've only gone twice, so we should make quite a pair."

"The only thing that should stand between you and the pins is the gutter," Gail teased.

Janet picked up a decorator pillow off the couch and threw it into the kitchen. "I don't know why I put up with you."

"I do," Gail commented saucily. "It's my Stroganoff. Come on, dinner's ready."

Janet parked in front of her parents' home an hour later. She saw the drapes move and knew that her brother had been at the window waiting for her arrival. A second later the front door flew open and Joel bounded down the porch stairs, running toward her. His young face was lit up with an inner glow of happiness.

"Hi, Janny," he greeted and threw his arms

16

around his sister, squeezing her with all the enthusiasm of his thirteen years.

Joel had the irritating habit of touching her hair and Janet gently lifted the eager fingers from the folds of her long brown curls. Returning the pressure of his hug, she asked, "Are you ready for our date?"

"Ready," he said, nodding his head emphatically.

"Let's go tell Mom and Dad we're leaving."

Joel hurried into the house ahead of her.

Leonora Montgomery looked up and laid her needlepoint aside when Janet walked in the house. "Hi, honey."

"Hi, Mom."

"Where are you two off to this week?" Stewart Montgomery was working at the dining room table. Bibles, commentaries and several other volumes littered the surface as he prepared Sunday's sermon. He was doing a series from the book of Romans.

"I thought we'd go bowling," Janet answered.

"Yippee," Joel shouted and ran into his bedroom, returning a minute later. "I want ice cream too," he said.

"We'll see," Janet replied.

"I said I want ice cream," Joel insisted. "I'll pay," he said and held out three dimes in the palm of his hand.

"In that case, little brother, you've got yourself a deal." She looped her arm through his and smiled back at her parents. "We'll be home in a couple of hours."

"Take your time, dear," her mother said, focusing her attention on the intricate needlepoint pattern.

Joel and Janet were enjoying their ice cream alfresco in the late summer evening when Janet happened to look into the street and notice the silver Mercedes. The musical laughter of the female occupant of the car drew attention away from the sleek lines of the vehicle. For a second, Janet almost choked on the praline delight ice cream. It was Reese Edwards and a new blonde. A chill gripped her, though it had nothing to do with what she was eating. She couldn't move, couldn't tear her eyes from the happy couple. What was the matter with her? What concern was it of hers if Reese Edwards chose to date empty-headed, inane women with identical looks and personalities? This one seemed pretty enough; they all were. But besides the model's figure, they all had a vocabulary so limited that Janet wondered if it went beyond the word "yes."

Janet had a hard time sleeping that night. Every time she closed her eyes she was haunted with the image of Reese in the arms of another blonde beauty. Why should she care if he dated and bedded a thousand women? What he shared with these women wasn't love, not in the way God intended it to be between a man and a woman. Why should it hurt so much to see him with another woman? The question seemed to demand an answer, but Janet could find none.

She woke with a headache and downed two aspirins with her juice and toast.

Gail noticed something was wrong almost immediately. "You don't look so hot. Are you sure you feel like going to work this morning?"

"I'm all right." She felt awful but was sure the aspirins would take effect in a short time.

Reese was at his desk when Janet entered the room, and the connecting door between the two offices was open.

"Morning, Janet," he greeted cheerfully.

Unbuttoning her blue jacket, she turned her back to him and mumbled, "Yes, it is, isn't it?" Following her usual morning routine, she put on a pot of coffee and brought him a cup when it had finished brewing.

He didn't glance up when she set the coffee mug on his desk. A look of total concentration furrowed his brow and Janet could almost picture his mind, spinning in channels she'd never hope to understand. Last night was the first time she had seen Reese with one of his women. She was all too aware of his dealings with the opposite sex. She ordered flowers for them, arranged for theater tickets and several times had purchased gifts. But last night was the first time she had actually viewed Reese with someone else. She still didn't understand why it had upset her so much. She thought she knew him so well, yet she didn't really know him at all. Janet smiled softly to herself. Ten minutes from now he'd probably look up, notice the coffee and wonder when she'd brought it.

Still tangled in the web of her thoughts, Janet didn't hear the door to the outer office open or see the figure emerge until she almost walked into the elderly gentleman.

"Oh dear, Mr. Edwards, I'm so sorry. I didn't see you."

A flickering smile touched the edges of his mouth. "That's quite all right. It's been several years since a lovely young woman threw herself into my arms."

Her laugh contained a nervous high tone as she stepped aside, but not before noticing Reese's appraisal of her. He looked slightly stunned, as if suddenly aware she was a woman. For two years he had seen her as a highly efficient secretary who oversaw the workings of his office, nothing more. She could have been a robot for all he knew. The headache she had woke with that morning throbbed with renewed intensity.

When Reese's father left the office a half hour later, Janet watched him go. Samuel Edwards was man aged beyond his years. His hair was completely white and he slouched forward slightly when he walked, as if carrying a heavy load on his shoulders. His eyes were as dark as his son's, yet they contained an intolerable sadness. He had established Dyna-Flow in the pre–World War II era and had made a name for himself by manufacturing small airplane parts. The company still handled several government contracts, but also sold parts to the major airplane builders.

Although Samuel Edwards was retired, he kept current with Dyna-Flow's dealings. Janet had never known Reese to hesitate when needing business advice. He went directly to his father when something was bothering him. She appreciated that about Reese. He wasn't so proud that he would not avail himself of his father's experience and business acumen.

They both were indebted to the elder Edwards. It was because of Samuel Edwards that Janet had the excellent job she did. Fresh out of secretarial school, she had been hired as a typist, one of many assistants to the vice president, Malcolm Hayes. She'd been in that position only six months when Mr. Hayes' secretary had taken a three-month leave of absence to have a baby. Janet had taken over the lead position in the interim. It was during that time that Reese's secretary, who had worked with his father for fifteen years, retired. Reese had gone through a rapid succession of replacements, the longest lasting three days. It wasn't that he was ill-tempered or abusive—he was exacting.

When he wanted something, he wanted it immediately. One of the girls who had walked out of his office claimed that Reese needed a psychic, or at least someone who could anticipate his needs.

It had been the elder Edwards who suggested Janet. Betty St. George, Malcolm's private secretary, had recently returned and Janet was pleased to have the opportunity.

The first days they'd worked together had not gone well. Twice within the first hour she'd considered handing in her notice. Reese was gruff and impatient, expecting Janet to intuitively know certain things. He accepted no excuses, not even ignorance. Several times she'd been tempted to empty the coffee pot over his head but had managed to restrain herself. Gradually she had learned that if she maintained her temper and presented a calm, cool facade when he made curt demands, she could cope.

At the end of her first two weeks, Reese had called her into his office and given her a large raise. At regular intervals in the following two years he had increased her salary, and Janet doubted there was any job she could have gotten that paid as well. It would never be easy to work for Reese, Janet realized, but there were personal rewards and plenty of satisfaction in knowing she was a vital part of keeping the office running smoothly.

The intercom buzzed, breaking into her thoughts. "I'm ready for you now, Janet." Her heart quickened at the sound of his voice. What was the matter with her lately? Their relationship had been cast two years before and remained strictly professional. She couldn't be nourishing any secret desire that Reese would notice her as a woman. Such thoughts were self-defeating. She wasn't his type; she wasn't even blonde. Respect and a certain amount of admiration were all she felt for Reese, she told herself forcefully as she pushed her glasses from the edge of her nose and reached for her pencil and pad.

The high-backed leather chair swiveled around as she entered his office. Again she felt his gaze sweep over her as if he were seeing her for the first time. Janet knew that at five eight she must look like an Amazon in comparison to the dainty, delicately boned women he preferred. Her dark hair was pulled away from her face and coiled in a chignon at the base of her neck. Her blue eyes, the color of the spring sky after a rainfall, were probably her best feature. But even these were disguised behind glasses with large frames. In deference to her position, Janet wore crisp business suits, linen in the summer and a wool blend in winter in a variety of blues and grays.

"Here." He seemed to snap himself from the introspection and handed Janet several cassettes from the Dictaphone. "Have these ready for me to

23

sign this afternoon," he said in a curt tone. "See if you can get tickets to the symphony for tomorrow night and have flowers sent to Bunny Jacobs." He rattled off an address. "Also get Henry on the phone for me."

"Did you say the flowers were for Bunny or Bubbles Jacobs." She didn't attempt to hide the snicker in her voice. In all the time Janet had worked for Reese she had never seen him look angrier. His fingers tightened around a pencil until the force of his grip snapped the wood in two.

"Bunny," he repeated.

Carefully she wrote down the name. "Is that everything?"

His eyes seemed to burn right through her; his mouth was pressed in a tight impatient line, as if he was restraining himself from saying something more.

Walking from the room, Janet paused in the doorway as the room began to spin. Her hand reached out to steady herself. She felt queasy and sick.

"Janet, are you all right?"

The tender concern in his voice made her want to cry. Numbly she shook her head. "I'm fine, just a little dizzy, that's all."

He placed an arm around her waist, lending her his support. "I knew something was wrong," he chuckled, "you didn't put any sugar in my coffee. I can't remember a time my efficient secretary forgot something as important as sugar in my coffee. Come on, I'm taking you home."

"No!" she protested immediately. The feel of his arm against her was doing erratic things to her heartbeat and she broke the contact. "I'll be fine in a minute. Really," she insisted again.

He released her, but helped her into her chair. "Fine or not, I'm taking you home. You shouldn't have even come in this morning."

Treacherous tears welled in her eyes. Reese hated weak women. Hadn't he just told her yesterday how much he detested a woman who cried? She buried her chin into her shoulder and sniffled. "Please . . . I'll take the bus home."

"Miss Montgomery, you don't honestly expect me to send you out on the streets looking like this," he argued. "You're so peaked someone's likely to mistake you for a ghost."

Lifting her glasses, she blotted the moisture from her cheeks. "If you're trying to make me feel better, then you're failing miserably."

His soft chuckle brought a weak smile trembling at the corners of her full mouth.

"Here, put this on." He handed her the jacket she'd worn that morning.

Janet accepted the coat. "What about—" She wasn't allowed to finish.

"I'll have someone else type it. As much as you may think otherwise, you're not completely indispensable."

Curious stares followed them out of the building. A hand placed protectively at the back of her waist added to the speculation. In two years Janet hadn't missed a day of work. Now that she was going to, it was to the amusement of the entire office staff. She felt her face grow crimson.

Reese unlocked the passenger door of the silver Mercedes. It was the same vehicle she'd seen him in the night before, and she bit into her upper lip as she climbed inside. Her hand ran over the smooth white seats, the feel of supple leather against her fingers. Janet couldn't help asking herself, How many other women have sat in this seat? How many other hearts has Reese broken? She gave a small gasp when she realized what her mind had questioned.

Reese cast her a worried look. "Are you okay?"

"Fine," she muttered and quickly turned her head to gaze out the side window. Other women? She wasn't one of his women, would never be in that elite group . . . how could her heart be involved? Quickly she shoved the thought from her mind.

". . . your address?" The question came at her unexpectedly. Janet hadn't been listening, too shocked at what her mind was saying to her.

She rolled off the street name and sat, hands clenched on her lap, as he manipulated the car through downtown Denver.

He pulled up in front of the apartment building

and, before she could protest, climbed out of the car and came around to her side.

The wind whipped soft wisps of hair about her face as she paused on the sidewalk. "I want to thank you . . ." she began. The hand tucked protectively under her elbow shocked her. She was almost lifted from the cement as she struggled to avoid his touch. "Really . . . there's no need to walk me to the door."

"I have something to discuss with you and I prefer to do it privately."

Janet conceded ungraciously and led the way to her apartment. The key slipped easily into the lock and she pushed open the door and stepped inside the tidy room. For the first time Janet was grateful for the arrangement she'd worked out with Gail. She did all the cleaning and Gail did the cooking and dishes. Gail openly admitted to being a slob, and if it were left to her, clothes would be littered across every available space of the apartment. If Reese was going to come into their apartment, at least he'd see it when it was neat and orderly.

His gaze did a sweeping inspection of the room, taking in details of the decor, which the girls called modern antiques.

The amusement in his look brought a questioning glance from Janet.

"Somehow I knew you'd live in a place where everything sparkles from the shine. I think the

27

phrase 'A place for everything and everything in its place' was created with you in mind."

Janet bristled. "I'm sure you didn't come here to discuss my housekeeping techniques."

"No, I didn't."

"Then what?" she prompted.

"I've noticed a certain reluctance on your part to discuss getting a word processor for the office," he began uneasily.

Janet shifted her feet, suddenly uncomfortable. "Not reluctance," she commented with a weak smile. "A gnawing fear would more aptly describe my feelings."

"Perhaps this wouldn't be the best time to discuss the subject."

"I think we'd better." Her knees felt unsteady and she lowered herself onto the overstuffed sofa with worn chocolate brown upholstery.

"I had dinner with a friend of mine yesterday. A computer expert. He was making some amazing statements about the amount of time that can be saved by one of these machines."

A prickling of apprehension raised goose bumps on her forearms. "You don't seem to understand."

He sat across from her in an olive green wingback chair. "What don't I understand?"

Janet pushed the stray hairs off her forehead. "It took me five years to learn how to tie my shoes." She stood and walked to the other side of the room. "I'm totally unmechanical. I can't even figure out how to use a hand-operated can opener."

Amusement formed grooves at the corners of his mouth.

"I don't find this the least bit funny," she snapped.

"It's not." But the laughter continued to dance in his eyes. "I'm not going to desert you in your hour of need."

"Am I supposed to find that comforting?"

He arched an arrogant brow. "Some women would."

"But not this woman," she denied vehemently.

The laughter died as his eyes hardened. "I'm afraid you're going to be forced to accept the change."

Janet's eyes rounded incredulously as her stomach muscles coiled into a hard knot. She might as well resign right now. There was no hope for her.

Chapter Two

"It seems to me," Stewart Montgomery said, rubbing his chin with his index finger and thumb, "that there's a verse someplace that says, 'I can do all things through Christ which strengtheneth me.'"

"Honestly, Dad"—Janet glared across the living room at her father—"sometimes I think having you know the Bible so well is the worst thing about being a preacher's kid."

"I'm a PK," Joel added proudly.

"Joel, why not give your sister the picture you made for her yesterday."

Her father's smile produced a heavy sigh from within Janet. No one seemed to understand her anxiety over having to face a computer Monday morning. Her family apparently had enough faith in her to believe she was capable of mastering anything. Unfortunately, Janet was more of a realist. She recognized her limitations, and lack of computer skills was one of them.

Joel appeared a minute later and handed her a piece of paper with meticulously drawn letters, decorated with flowers. The paper said: THE LORD NEVER PANICS.

"See, Janny, see what I made for you?" Joel handed it to her, pulling her face to the side so she would concentrate on him alone.

Janet accepted the paper and read over the message. Each time the truth of her father's assurances became more real. The tension seemed to ease from her. Her thirteen-year-old brother was right. Again Joel's uncomplicated faith had touched her.

Janet brought the sign to work with her Monday morning. Pausing in the doorway of her office she noted that her trusted typewriter had been moved to a side table at the right of her desk. The computer, with its small screen, rested prominently on the desktop. A large printer sat beside it. Already her hands felt clammy and her heart hammered like she'd just completed a six-mile run.

"Don't look so frightened." Reese's voice came out of nowhere and Janet looked up, startled.

"I'm not," she said and could have kicked herself for the telltale tremble in her voice.

A thick brow was raised in mockery. "I promise it won't bite."

"Wonderful," she murmured sarcastically. "Am I supposed to applaud?"

"No," he said without emotion. "That comes later."

Ignoring Reese as best she could, Janet pulled out the bottom desk drawer and somehow managed to keep her hands from shaking.

"I've enrolled you in computer classes beginning tonight," Reese told her, planting his hands against her desk. "I'll be attending with you. That way, if you have any problems I should be able to help you."

Reese's thoughtfulness surprised her. "I appreciate that." Her blue eyes lifted to his face and her gaze was held by his. Something she couldn't decipher flickered from the depth of his eyes and he glanced away.

"How . . . how long will the classes be?" Her voice sounded strange, weak, as if she had tried to swallow and speak at the same time.

"Every night this week. Is that going to be a problem?"

She shook her head. "No, except for Thursday. I have plans Thursday night." It would be easy enough to find a replacement for her Wednesday night class at church, but she wouldn't disappoint Joel. She'd promised to take him to a Walt Disney movie and keeping her promise to her younger brother had priority.

"I'll see about arrangements to make up that one class then," Reese said and turned. Halfway into his office, he paused and came back. "How long have you been working for me, Janet?"

Again she looked up, surprised. "Two years."

"Really?" He arched both brows expressively. "You're not due for a raise, are you?"

"No, you gave me one three months ago."

"Yes, I remember that now," he replied smoothly and retreated into his office.

Janet watched him go with confused emotions. She had the strangest sensation that for some unknown reason Reese had noticed her for the first time. For two years she had blended into the background so completely that he was barely aware she was around. Shrugging lightly, she put on a pot of coffee. She had no complaints regarding the lack of attention he gave her. It was a good secretary's job to blend into the background.

Bunny Jacobs phoned for Reese late that

morning. Her voice was soft and purring and Janet had to squelch the unreasonable rise of impatience she felt at having to deal with another of Reese's women. He had asked her to hold all calls, but this usually didn't include his consorts. Rather than risk his ire, she said, "If you'll hold the line I'll see if he's in. Bunny's on line one," she spoke into the intercom.

"I thought I said to hold all calls."

Janet expelled an unsteady breath. "I wasn't sure if—"

"I'll take the call." The communication was cut off abruptly.

Janet heard him pick up the receiver. The tone of his voice altered to a more caressing sound. "I can't tonight."

With the connecting door partially ajar, Janet was an unwilling eavesdropper. She stood, retreating to the far side of the room in an effort to avoid hearing the conversation. It always troubled her when she was forced to listen to the soft caressing tone of Reese's voice when he spoke to one of his blondes. She knew she was being unreasonable, but logic seemed beyond her lately, especially where Reese was concerned.

"You know I'd rather be with you . . ."

Clenching her hands at her side, Janet swallowed tightly and walked out of the office.

When she returned five minutes later the connecting door was securely shut and a terse note was on her desk that read: HOLD ALL CALLS.

To avoid looking at the computer, Janet worked the rest of the morning from her typewriter. Gail entered the office at noon to remind Janet it was time for their lunch break.

"Gee," she said, studying the top of Janet's desk. "The computer doesn't look like such a beast."

Janet looked up and laughed sarcastically. "It can't be much of a monster when I haven't turned it on yet."

Gail's mouth dropped open. "You mean to say it's been sitting here all morning and you haven't even turned it on?"

Miserably Janet nodded.

"Why not?"

"I couldn't find the switch."

Her friend's voice softened at the distress etched so clearly in Janet's face.

Gail immediately plopped herself into the chair. "Well, it's got to be here someplace." Agile fingers ran over the top of the keys, seeking some clue.

"Just look at all those keys," Janet said with a rising sense of panic. "System controls, file controls, applications and typestyles, and that's just the top row. And I can't even manage to figure out how to turn it on."

"The switch is on the side of the power unit."

Both girls jumped at the unexpected sound of Reese's voice. A rush of hot color suffused Janet's face as she turned around, making her resemble a guilty child.

"I'd demonstrate how it works, but the disks need to be formatted," he said, his voice laced with indulgent amusement. "I wouldn't want to take up any more of your lunch hour."

Their eyes met across the short space of the office. Janet had missed countless lunches typing urgent reports, letters and any number of things Reese needed in a rush. He hadn't been concerned about her missing her lunch then. But now the look in his eyes all but stopped her heartbeat.

"He's right," Gail interjected, "we'd better rush, or we won't get a table."

Janet lowered her gaze guiltily. She wished she could understand what was happening between Reese and her. In the space of a few days everything was different. And yet there was no logical explanation for the change.

Janet wore a skirt that night with a cranberry-colored blouse that had ruffles at the yoke. Uncoiling her hair, she brushed it until it shimmered and curled attractively around her soft shoulders. The rich chestnut-colored hair was a striking contrast to her piercing blue eyes. A single strand of delicately laced gold graced her neck. It bothered Janet that she was taking so much trouble to look her best for a computer class. Or was it for Reese?

Gail sauntered into the living room munching on

an apple and paused in midstride. "Wow." She gulped. "You look like dynamite."

"Explosive or destructive?"

Gail shrugged. "I don't know, but I have the distinct impression Mr. Edwards isn't going to know who you are."

"Oh, Gail, honestly." Janet moved her hand expressively. "I've worked with him every day for two years; of course he'll recognize me." She paused momentarily to wonder if Reese had ever seen her with her hair down, or when she wasn't wearing her glasses. Not that he'd notice. Maybe if she was blonde and six inches shorter, she mused.

Reese arrived promptly at 6:45. Gail answered the front door as Janet took her beige blazer from the hall closet. Although it was the first week of September there was already a chill to the evening air.

"Janet?" There was a questioning note in the low-pitched voice.

"What did I tell you?" Gail mumbled as she stepped aside.

"Hi." Janet managed a smile as her hand tightened around the purse handle. Reese had dressed casually in a navy turtleneck sweater and sport coat that openly reminded her of the leashed strength and power of the man. There could be no denying that Reese Edwards was a dynamic man. His looks were so compelling that for a crazy moment Janet couldn't take her eyes off him.

"Shall we go?"

The voice snapped her back into reality. "Yes . . . of course."

He opened the car door for her and Janet climbed inside. "Once I know how to get to the classes I can meet you there," she said with an unsteady breath. "There's no reason for you to come out of your way to pick me up."

"I don't mind." He dismissed her suggestion and focused his concentration on the road ahead.

The class was specially designed for executive secretaries and their employers. Mostly smaller businesses were involved. From the conversation exchanged between the instructor and another executive, Janet learned that the Simplex, the computer Reese had purchased, was said to be the least complicated of all computers sold. She smiled at Reese gratefully.

The first hour of the course was spent relating the history of computers and the revolution taking place around the world because of the possibilities and capabilities of the small machine. The last half hour was used to familiarize the group with computer lingo. A hands-on experience was promised for the next evening's class.

"It's not so terrifying, is it?" Reese asked as they walked toward the parked car.

"I'll reserve my judgment until after this week," Janet replied.

Reese stopped, hands in his pockets. "Do you

always stand back and analyze something before making a decision?"

"I suppose so." His question struck a raw nerve and she stiffened slightly. "I'm not often carried away with emotion, if that's what you're asking." A thousand times Janet wished she could be more like Gail, who leaped into madcap schemes and came out better for the experience. Gail could walk into a store, pick something haphazardly off the rack and look like she'd spent weeks looking for just the perfect match. Janet sometimes agonized over the simplest things; she wished she were different, but her sense of order and her tendency toward perfection made her prudent.

"Coffee?" Reese asked. But before she could respond, he pulled into the parking lot of an all-night restaurant.

Janet slid into the red booth and Reese sat opposite her. When the waitress came for their order he looked up and smiled impersonally. "A piece of apple pie, à la mode, and coffee for the lady."

"Reese," she whispered fiercely. "What are you doing?"

"Nothing, why?" He looked perplexed. The girl began to step away.

"Miss," Janet called her back.

"Yes?" The voice was laced with impatience.

"I'd like a piece of pie too."

The girl glanced from one to the other. "Are you sure?"

"Very," Janet murmured. When the waitress had moved out of hearing distance, Janet leaned forward, her eyes sparking fire. "What did you do that for? I'm perfectly capable of deciding what I want to order."

Elbows resting on the table, Reese eased his upper torso forward until their faces were separated by only a few inches. "Why are we whispering?" he asked.

Straightening, Janet glared at him, exasperated. "Are you always this difficult."

"No," he assured her with a crooked grin. "I guess I owe you an apology. The women I usually date are afraid to order lettuce for fear of gaining weight. I should have realized you'd be different."

"Oh." Janet wasn't sure if that was a compliment or not. She was different all right; the women Reese dated were the epitome of delicate, gentle femininity. "If you ever took out a woman taller than five feet you'd realize that girls as tall as I am can eat more," she replied flippantly.

Reese's eyes narrowed, his expression hauntingly cool.

Their order arrived and Janet had to force herself to eat the ice cream. The frozen dessert seemed to spread its chill all the way from her stomach up to her heart. She noticed that Reese didn't seem any more interested in eating than she did. After a few minutes of stilted silence, he picked up the tab and left the booth to pay their bill.

He drove to Janet's apartment, neither of them saying a word, and eased the car alongside the curb.

"Good night, Miss Montgomery." The upward curve of his mouth was humorless.

Her hand on the door handle, Janet nearly leaped from the car.

He waited until she had unlocked the apartment door and turned to wave, signaling that everything was okay.

When Janet arrived at the office the next morning, Reese was sitting at her computer, his concentration intent as he read from the instruction manual. Little red lights were flashing from the disk drives at the base of the machine and Janet stood back, watching them flash off and on while a soft grinding sound was emitted from the base of the computer. It was several seconds before Reese noticed that she was there.

"Good morning," she greeted him stiffly.

"I'm getting the disks ready for you to use."

Janet stood back and nodded. She had learned in the class the night before that the disks needed to be divided into tracts to save the data she would be storing. The technical term was called formatting.

Busying herself by hanging up her coat, putting

on the first pot of coffee and sorting through the mail, Janet did her best to ignore the fact that Reese was occupying her desk.

"Miss Montgomery." Reese was calling her. He didn't follow any real pattern; sometimes he called her Janet and other times by her surname. Lately, however, he'd most commonly called her Janet, at least until last night.

"Yes?"

"Sit down," he instructed, standing and pulling out her chair.

Janet did as he requested.

Hands on the back of the chair, Reese rolled her toward the desk. "Type the following memo," he said crisply.

Immediately Janet went to scoot back to get to the typewriter.

"No," he stopped her, "type it into the computer."

Her hands froze and she looked back at him, her eyes filled with panic. "Not yet, I don't know anything about this thing, I might do something wrong."

"It wouldn't surprise me, but do it anyway."

Holding her back straight, she lightly placed her fingers on the keyboard. Other than several rows of keys to the left and right of the main section, it looked and felt like a typewriter.

Reese rattled off several sentences. Instinct took over and Janet typed with all the speed and dexterity she was accustomed to having on her old electric typewriter.

Pleased with herself, she placed her hands on her lap when she'd finished.

"Not bad." Reese patted her shoulder, and where his hand touched, a flowing warmth seemed to spread until it reached all the way to the tips of her fingers. Leaning forward slightly, his head almost next to hers, Reese read the monitor screen.

Janet could smell the manly scent of his after-shave, which disturbed her all the more.

"You misspelled 'employees.'"

The criticism brought her attention sharply back to where it belonged. "I did not," she denied, without knowing if she had or not.

"No, you didn't," Reese agreed, his voice full of teasing humor. "But let's pretend you did."

"I think you should be aware that I placed fifth in the state-wide spelling bee when I was eleven."

His soft chuckle stirred the hairs at the side of her face. "I would have guessed as much."

"All right, I'll play your little game and pretend I misspelled a word."

"Let's correct it then." It took five minutes for Janet to correct one word, which would have taken five seconds on her typewriter, but she restrained herself from telling him as much. By the time they'd finished, the phone was ringing and the start of another workday couldn't be delayed.

Reese picked her up that evening the same time he had the night before. The instructor had them both work with the computer while he explained the simplest functions. Nonetheless, by the time class was over, Janet's head was spinning with information. Reese drove her directly home. She couldn't prevent a soft sigh of disappointment when he drove away.

Gail was sprawled across the sofa, reading, when Janet let herself into the apartment.

"You're home early," she said, glancing up from the magazine. Unhooking her foot from the back of the couch, she sat upright.

"We didn't stop for coffee tonight," Janet explained and yawned. "I'm tired. I think I'll get ready for bed." She wasn't fooling Gail; she was avoiding discussing Reese and they both knew it.

Janet attacked her teeth with the toothbrush, angry with herself. All this new awareness of Reese as a man, all these strange feelings she was experiencing were at the surface, ready for her to deal with. Yet she refused. She didn't want to think about Reese in any other capacity except as her boss. Staring at herself in the mirror, Janet was forced to admit she wouldn't allow herself to think about him, she couldn't, she was afraid.

Wednesday followed the pattern of the two previous days and nights. Reese was unusually quiet on the way home from class. Because Janet was taking the class and learning how the Simplex

43

operated bit by bit each night, the computer didn't strike the terror in her heart it once did. Comparing the Simplex to some of the others, Janet was impressed with the simplicity of its operation.

"This may sound strange after only three nights of classes, but I'm beginning to feel a little more confident. I think once I learn all the controls, I shouldn't have too much trouble effectively operating a computer."

Reese's gaze moved from the road and flickered over her. "I knew you would. At the same time I think it's important for you to complete the course."

"I agree."

"You still can't come tomorrow night?" He made the question more of an accusation.

"No, I wish I could."

"What's so important that's going on tomorrow?" He sounded almost angry and Janet glanced at him curiously.

"You won't believe this, but it's a movie."

"I suspect it's not so much the show but the company you'll be keeping."

Janet couldn't deny it; her relationship with Joel was very special to her. Besides, she'd seen *Snow White and the Seven Dwarfs* three times. "You're right, would you like to know what movie I'm seeing?"

"No, I wouldn't," he said tersely.

His hands tightened around the steering wheel and Janet watched him with a growing confusion as he sped ahead. It was almost as if he couldn't get her out of his car fast enough; as if he wanted to avoid her company. She shrugged her shoulders when he dropped her off at the apartment and drove away. The night before he'd walked her to the door and Monday, even when he was angry, he'd waited until she was safely inside her apartment before driving off. If she didn't know any better, she'd think he was jealous. The likelihood was so obscure that Janet couldn't prevent a smile.

Reese's mood hadn't improved much by the following morning. He responded to her good-morning with an impatient grunt and immediately began making demands. For an instant she was tempted to remind him she didn't officially start work for another ten minutes. Instead she got Malcolm Hayes on the phone and brought in the files he requested.

By ten o'clock he'd snapped at her twice and threw a tantrum when he couldn't find a file he needed. Forcing herself to stay calm, she sorted through the stacks on his desk and discovered the missing file within minutes. Reese's thank-you was barely civil.

Janet couldn't remember a day she was more anxious to leave the office. It wasn't that he hadn't had these moods in the past; he had. The last time had been when a shipment of urgently needed parts for a government contract was lost in transit. But there was nothing wrong at the office or at any of the plants that she knew about.

After showering and changing clothes, Janet drove to her parents' home. As usual, Joel was at the window watching for her and raced out the door the minute she pulled into the driveway.

"Hi, Janny." His smile was filled with warmth, and Janet noted how he struggled to keep himself from reaching for her hair. "Did you use my picture?"

"I sure did," she beamed. "And you're right, you know. When we have Jesus in our hearts we shouldn't panic."

His boyish head bobbed. "I know," he said simply.

Their father looked up from the newspaper he was reading when Janet and Joel walked into the living room. "How's my daughter the computer expert?"

"Fine." She sat down on the ottoman in front of him. "Do you remember in the sermon Sunday how you talked about Christians being a living sacrifice to God?"

"Yes." He lowered the paper.

"I've been thinking about what you said, Dad, and decided there's one basic problem with that."

"Oh?" Stewart Montgomery's eyes grew serious.

Janet knew what he was thinking. Her faith in God and her acceptance of Christ had not been an easy thing in her life. Since she'd been raised as a preacher's kid, so much had been expected of her by her parents and the congregation. It wasn't a role Janet had slipped into easily and she hadn't made a complete commitment to Christ until her late teens.

"Yes," she said and smiled. "I've learned that the problem with my being a living sacrifice to God is that I keep crawling off the altar."

Her father's chuckle filled the living room. "I think that's a problem for many of us."

Joel laughed too, although Janet was aware he probably didn't fully understand what she had said.

"The movie's over at eight, so I'll have Joel back early tonight," she told her mom on the way out the door.

"Don't let him have too much junk food," Leonora warned as she stood in the doorway and watched them leave.

The apartment was empty by the time Janet returned at eight-thirty. Gail had a dinner date with Ben Gavin, a city accountant and Janet knew not to expect her until late. Gail had been seeing a lot of Ben lately and she was aware that the relationship between the two was developing nicely. Lucky Gail, she thought as she poured herself a glass of milk and propped her shoeless feet on the kitchen chair opposite her. Currently there wasn't anyone special in her life. She hadn't seen Gary in several weeks; she liked him and realized that, given time, their feelings for one another could eventually grow into love. Gary was everything she should want in a husband. He was committed to Christ and the church; he had a good job and a bright future. Was she immature to expect something more? Sighing, she placed the empty glass in the kitchen sink. The trouble was, she didn't know what to expect.

The doorbell chimed and Janet frowned, glancing at the clock. Who would be coming this late?

Looking through the peephole, Janet's blue eyes rounded incredulously as she saw Reese standing outside her door, hands in his pockets. He looked even more surprised than she when Janet opened the door.

"Reese."

"Hello, Janet."

"Hi." She needed the support of the door to stand upright. After a day like today she thought he'd come to complain about some of her work. But one look told her that wasn't it.

He shifted his weight from one foot onto the other. "Can I come in?"

"Yes . . . of course." She stepped aside.

"I didn't know if you'd be home."

"Yes . . . yes, I am," she responded and could

have groaned at the stupidity of the remark. More than anyone she had ever known, Reese could reduce her to a childish level. He might see her as analytical and logical, but around him she behaved like a schoolgirl, especially these last two weeks. It had been only from habit that she'd been able to maintain a business attitude during office hours.

His look was strangely brooding and Janet lowered her eyes under the force of his.

"Is something wrong . . . at the office, I mean."

"No, what could be wrong there?"

"You tell me. You created enough enemies today." She stood with her hands behind her.

"Are you my enemy, Janet?" he asked her dryly.

She shook her head, her emotions muddled by his advancing closeness. "No, I'm used to you." Now for every step he took toward her, she took one in retreat. "Can I get you anything? There's hot water for coffee and I think there's a Pepsi in the fridge."

"No thanks."

"Would you like to sit down?" she offered politely.

He smiled his thanks and sat in the chair. Janet sat across from him on the couch, perching on the edge of the cushion. "I suppose you're wondering why I've come."

"No," she denied, then shook her head. "Well, yes, I guess I am."

"First I want to apologize for my behavior today. I was in a foul mood and took out my temper on you."

"That's all right, we all have an off day now and then."

He dismissed her easy acceptance of his apology with an angry shake of his head and clenched his hands together in front of him as he leaned forward. "And second, I thought you'd like to know what went on in class tonight."

Janet relaxed and responded with an eager nod. "Yes, I would."

Reese's dark eyes smiled into hers. The lines around his mouth deepened into grooves. "I took good notes." He pulled several bits and pieces of paper from the pocket of his sports coat and handed them to her.

Janet laughed as she accepted the scraps. "Honestly, Reese, how am I supposed to make heads or tails out of this mess."

"Here, let me help." He stood, walking around the coffee table to sit beside her. The sofa accepted his weight as he sat so close their thighs touched. Janet's hands trembled slightly as she handed him back the notes.

"We reviewed the control commands," he began. "It's not all that disorganized. I made notes on a separate piece of paper for each command. Here, let's look at this one first." He placed the torn corner of a page on the table in front of them.

"To bring up the Block menu, all that needs to be done is to push the control button and the letter *b*."

"That sounds simple enough," she agreed. "But what does the Block menu do?" She straightened and looked up at him.

Reese straightened. Their eyes met; his mouth was only inches from hers. "That's . . . easy . . . to . . ." His hand reached out to lift the hair off her shoulder, "remember," he finished. His hand rested on the gentle curve of her shoulder; his eyes continued to hold hers.

Janet wanted to look away, break the spell of this craziness, but she couldn't. Her mouth trembled as his hand moved from her shoulder to the side of her neck, stroking the thickness of her long hair.

Hesitantly, as if in slow motion, his mouth descended toward hers. The feather-light touch of his lips settling over hers was more of a caress than a kiss, as though he were as unsure as she.

Breaking the contact, Reese slowly pulled away. Their eyes met and locked for a breathless moment. Janet stared at him, surprised, uncertain, and read the same doubts in his features. The hammering pulse at the side of her neck seemed to attract his attention and his gaze shifted to her throat.

Janet offered no resistance when his strong fingers cupped her shoulders, directing her toward him. Of their own accord, her hands slipped around his neck, and she moaned softly in surrender as his mouth parted hers.

Expelling a shuddering breath, Reese buried his face in the hollow of her throat, spreading tiny kisses there as she fought to compose herself.

"Reese," she whispered, breaking the contact. "What's happening to us?"

Chapter Three

"You look very prim and proper this morning," Gail mentioned over the breakfast table.

Janet's hand tested the hair at the base of her neck. She had tightly twisted it into place this morning and chosen her least attractive business suit. She didn't know what was happening between her and Reese, but it had to stop immediately.

He had kissed her three times last night. Each kiss deeper, more demanding, sapping her strength to resist. Breathlessly she had pulled herself out of his arms and walked to the other side of the room. Reese had come to stand behind her, slowly bringing her close as his mouth sought the gentle slope of her neck.

"I don't know what's happening," he had whispered. "I don't want to know."

"If you leave the notes from class," she'd said, fighting to keep her voice even, "I'll look them over before work tomorrow."

Reese froze, his fingers exerting a slight pressure on her shoulders as he turned her around. "Is that the way you want it?" His gaze bore into hers, then gradually lowered to rest on lips that felt swollen from his plundering kisses.

"Yes," she shook her head emphatically. "Yes, please."

Reese had inhaled deeply, grabbed his jacket from the back of the sofa and stalked out the door.

Janet hadn't slept, tossing for hours as she struggled with the events of the night. Her working relationship with Reese would be ruined if she didn't show more self-restraint. Reese didn't look as if he was willing to keep things under control. What had changed? Had she suddenly flashed Reese an invisible green light? Nothing seemed to make sense, least of all her own feelings. She knew him too well, knew how he treated his women, knew what would happen to her if this continued.

"You ready?" Gail wore her sweater jacket and had taken her car keys from her purse. They took turns driving each week. If one was forced to work late, then the other took the bus home.

"Ready." Janet swung the purse strap over her shoulder and gave an unconscious sigh. Things would be strictly professional today, and from here on in.

Following routine, she hung up her coat, placed her purse in the bottom desk drawer and made coffee. Reese was already in his office, the adjoining door closed. Twenty minutes after her arrival Janet took in Reese's coffee. He didn't glance up and she was grateful.

"Good morning, Janet."

Her heartbeat accelerated briefly. "Good morning, Mr. Edwards," she responded crisply.

At her brittle tone, Reese diverted his attention from the file he was studying and raised his eyes to her. One brow quirked upward.

Janet's gaze avoided his. "Is there anything else?" she questioned with the same chilling politeness.

"Nothing," he replied, his voice slightly mocking.

Pride dictated that she hold her head high, her chin tilted at a stern angle, as she walked out the door, closing it firmly.

Reese came out of his office midmorning to give her some reports to type, saying he needed them by that afternoon. He left soon after for a meeting. Their hands brushed as she accepted the folder and a firelike sensation shot up her arm. Janet was forced to swallow tightly to maintain her poise.

"Janet."

She pushed her glasses up from the tip of her nose and glanced upward.

"Use the computer, understand?"

She hoped to hide the panic in her eyes and nodded. "If you insist."

"I do." The steel hardness in his voice seemed to reach out and assault her.

A half hour later, she wheeled her chair in front of the Simplex. The operating manual rested in her lap. The necessary steps to turn on the machine and bring up the editing mode were familiar enough for her to work confidently.

The report didn't contain columns of figures or other complicated data, but it was several pages in length and Janet hadn't done anything but the briefest documents on the Simplex.

Glancing at her watch, she noted that she should be able to complete the report by lunch if she was free to work without interruptions.

Her hands felt uncomfortable on the unfamiliar keyboard and her typing speed slowed, but soon her confidence grew and her fingers flew, setting a regular pace. Perhaps Reese was right, a computer was a miracle of modern technology, not some diabolical beast. The phone rang several times, but by noon Janet had almost finished. It certainly was easier not to have to stop and feed paper into the computer, as would have been necessary with a typewriter.

Pausing to flip to the last page of Reese's almost indecipherable handwriting, Janet looked up and noticed that the screen was blank.

For a second all she could do was stare at it in bewilderment. What had happened? Where did the report go? Had she typed the wrong button and caused this? After staring at the empty screen for a full five minutes, Janet reached for the user manual. Nothing that might be a possible explanation was listed. She pushed and pried every button.

"Is that report ready yet?" Reese sauntered into the office. When she didn't answer him right away, he asked her again. "Janet, I need the Phelps report."

"I don't have it," she snapped, while her eyes glinted, ready for battle. "Your precious computer ate it."

"What do you mean?" he demanded. "What did you do?"

"I didn't do anything," she insisted and sharply inhaled a shaky breath to hide the abject frustration. "I was almost done and suddenly the screen went blank. I've tried everything I know to retrieve it, but nothing's worked."

"You must have done something wrong."

"I didn't," she stormed. "It . . . just vanished." She threw her hands into the air. "Poof, gone . . ."

The hard line of his mouth tightened impatiently. "Perhaps if you had attended last night's class you would know how to deal with situations like this."

Pressing her lips together to prevent an angry retort, she said as evenly as possible, "If you'll excuse me." Extracting her purse from the desk, she scooted out of the chair and stood. "It's my lunch hour."

"What about the report?" The control Reese had on his anger sounded as thin as Janet's.

"The computer has it," she stated calmly and walked out the door.

An hour later, her temper under control due to Gail's calming influence, Janet returned to the office. Reese was sitting in her chair working at the computer. Resentment flared momentarily. Apparently he persisted in the belief she had done something wrong.

"Well?" she asked curtly.

He looked up as if surprised she was there. "My apologies, Janet. I phoned the computer store to see if they could explain what happened. It seems we experienced a power surge. I've ordered an adapter that will correct the problem in the future."

"I didn't think it was anything I'd done." Relief thickly coated her words.

"Does that mean you're willing to admit it *may* have been your fault?" His smile was potent enough to churn her stomach.

She flushed, feeling the rise of color flow into her cheeks. "Not exactly, but I couldn't very well deny the possibility." She averted her attention by replacing her purse in the desk. "I'll have the report for you as soon as possible."

Reese glanced at his watch. "I'll be out of the office for the rest of the afternoon. Malcolm will take care of it for me if you see to it that he gets it before five."

Janet nodded. "Fine."

"I'll pick you up at your place tonight at the regular time for class."

"I'll be ready."

Reese returned to his office to place a call. While he was still on the phone Bunny Jacobs came into the office. Dressed in a loose-fitting shimmering gold dress that looked like silk, she wore an endearing smile that brightened her beautiful blue eyes.

"Is Reese in?" She purred the question and gently swung the matching stole across one shoulder.

If Janet hadn't seen it a hundred times before, she could have laughed. There wasn't anyone in the world more empty-headed than this blonde. No one was that dumb; it had to be an act. The voice, the walk, the way Bunny dressed was so stereotyped it was unbelievable. Either this woman was genuine, or she was very shrewd. She knew what Reese Edwards liked and had perfected the role.

"Mr. Edwards is on the phone. Would you care to sit down and wait?" Janet offered politely. "There's coffee if you'd like a cup."

"Oh no," Bunny said, smiling sweetly. "I only drink natural things like orange juice and Coke. Coffee's supposed to be terrible for you."

"I read that too," Janet replied, doing her best to keep from making a sarcastic comment. Was this girl for real?

Bunny glanced at the closed door connecting the rooms. "Have you worked long for Reese?"

"Two years," Janet replied.

"I bet he's a wonderful boss." Bunny crossed one beautifully shaped leg across the other.

Janet could see no reason to disillusion the blonde. "Oh, he is."

"Since I've been dating Reese I've come to believe in love. It's just like the song . . . even the nights are better," she said with an exaggerated sigh.

Knowing the way Reese operated, Janet had to bite her lip from commenting that the nights were probably one of the first things to improve.

"He's got this dreadful meeting he must go to tonight and just couldn't bear the thought of a Friday without seeing me. He insisted on taking me out this afternoon. He is so . . . so . . ." She seemed to be searching for the right word.

"Wonderful?" Janet inserted.

"Oh yes, wonderful."

The extinguished light on the phone indicated Reese had finished his call. "If you'll excuse me a minute, I'll let Mr. Edwards know you're here."

"Of course." Bunny's perfectly formed mouth curved into an appreciative smile.

Rolling her chair away from her desk, Janet stood and tapped politely on the closed door before entering his office. Reese looked up expectantly, his gaze lazy and welcoming.

Her eyes met his look, her smile saccharine sweet as she murmured suggestively, "Bubbles Boom Boom is waiting." She didn't wait for his reaction, but turned to exit as quickly as possible.

Janet waited until Reese was in the outer office before stiffly informing him she'd see herself to the computer class. What was the matter with her? With one breath she was chastising herself for her un-Christian behavior and with the next deliberately baiting Reese.

"Is Miss Montgomery attending that dreadful meeting with you?" Bunny asked, her eyes wide and innocent as she looked at Reese, but Janet noted that as they came to rest on her they narrowed slightly as she studied Janet. Bunny stood and placed a hand in the crook of Reese's elbow.

Reese ignored Bunny's question. "I'll pick you up at your place, Miss Montgomery." His tone brooked no argument, but Janet chose to ignore him as she returned to her desk and purposely sat with her back to the couple. As far as Janet was concerned, they deserved one another.

She could almost feel Reese's eyes digging holes into her back. The tension between them was as tight and fine as a precision instrument.

Apparently Bunny was oblivious to it all, as Janet heard her coo lovingly, "We'll be late for our reservation if we don't hurry."

As soon as the office door clicked, indicating

that Reese and Bunny had left, Janet rolled her chair to her trusted typewriter in order to type the report. Her fingers were actually trembling as she placed them over the keys.

Never in all the years she'd worked for Reese had she spoken to him in anything but a dignified and professional manner. The change in their relationship was so drastic that for the first time Janet realized there was no going back. That impersonal business camaraderie was lost forever.

Janet spent a good portion of the afternoon typing the report. She made several typing errors, something she rarely did. While proofreading she discovered two misspellings. She hadn't misspelled anything in ten years.

Gail and Ben dated regularly on Friday nights, so Janet was alone when Reese rang the doorbell. Her hand froze as she replaced a stray strand from her chignon and paused to compose herself before opening the door. She hadn't changed clothes after work, choosing to remain in her business suit with her hair tightly coiled.

Reese's features were grim, his mouth a narrow slit. One look at the piercing eyes and Janet knew he had been waiting to speak to her from the minute he'd walked out of his office that afternoon. The apartment door closed ominously.

"Before you say anything," she murmured, her

hands folded neatly in front of her skirt. "I'd like to apologize for this afternoon." She hesitated. "My behavior was inexcusable." Janet sincerely regretted what she'd said, but the apology was issued as a desperate attempt to restore an amicable working relationship.

Reese did nothing to lessen her discomfort.

"I . . . I should never have spoken to you like that. I can only apologize."

"Is that all you have to say?" Reese demanded quietly.

Janet nodded her head, forcing herself to meet his eyes.

He was quiet for so long that Janet swallowed tightly. He was doing this on purpose, prolonging her discomfort, and she felt annoyed at him for being so arrogant.

He was studying her, his gaze lingering on her softly parted lips for a heart-stopping moment. "All right, let's forget the whole thing. Now I'll wait here for you to change your clothes."

"I was planning to go like this." Her hand made a weak, dismissive gesture.

Reese's gaze hardened. A frown drew his thick brows together as he slumped into the sofa. "For once, Miss Montgomery, humor me and change your clothes."

For the first time Janet noted the tired lines that fanned out like crow's-feet from his eyes and the dark shadows that were beginning to form.

"All right," she breathed. "I'll only be a minute." In order to save time, Janet removed the crisp white blouse and blazer jacket and replaced them with a soft pink pullover sweater. The transformation from a business suit to a casual outfit was a matter of a few simple changes. Unloosening her hair, Janet ran a quick brush through the long tendrils until they curled uniformly about her shoulders.

He stood when she entered the living room. "Much better," he murmured under his breath.

Janet bristled. Without her work clothes she felt more vulnerable to Reese's powerful masculinity. She had been immune to it for so long that now it seemed to hit her with hurricane force. Nervously she tucked a piece of hair around her ear. "I'll get my jacket."

Reese moved behind her as she took the coat from the hall closet. When she turned he was standing close enough to touch. Inhaling a sharp breath, Janet moved a step back. His mouth tightened in angry response as he took the coat out of her hand and held it open. Incapable of meeting his sharp gaze, Janet turned and slipped her arms into both sleeves at the same time. Reese slid the jacket into place; his hands cupped her shoulders, lingering a moment longer than necessary.

He remained strangely quiet during the drive to class, seemingly preoccupied. He pulled into a parking place on Colfax Avenue and switched off the engine. Turning, his gaze brushed over her face. "We've worked together for two years now, haven't we?"

"Yes," Janet nodded, stressing the affirmative.

He shifted in the seat so he could look at her. "You're valuable to me, Janet. I don't want to lose you. I know I can be an ill-tempered boor on occasion, impatient and irritable. But you've managed to withstand my moods and keep the office running smoothly. Without you I fear the company would look exactly like the top of my desk."

"I think you overestimate my talents, Mr. Edwards. I doubt that there's much that could be worse than your desk." She attempted to joke, but her fingers coiling around the strap of her purse betrayed her nerves. "I enjoy working at Dyna-Flow, and my salary is generous."

"I only pay people what they're worth." His hands firmly gripped the steering wheel. "I know this may sound like an unusual question, but can we start again?"

The conversation had been leading up to this point. Apparently Reese had as many questions about this thing between them as she did. They couldn't return to the impersonal business relationship that had existed for two years, but romantic involvement between them was equally impossible. She was an asset to his business and he knew it. Things needed to be brought into the open and Reese had chosen to do it now. Janet was grateful.

"I think we'd better," she said and smiled.

"Good."

Things did improve almost immediately. Everything was better.

Her mother noticed a change in Janet the following week when she picked up Joel for their regular outing.

"You've changed your hairstyle, haven't you, dear?" Leonora Montgomery questioned.

Janet looked up, surprised. "No, I've been wearing it like this for three years."

"Oh," she paused and tilted her head to examine her daughter again. "Something's different."

Janet couldn't think of a way to explain.

"It's in your face," her mother persisted. "It seems to shine. Is it a new kind of makeup?"

Janet nodded, hoping her mother would forgive her for avoiding the real reason. "Yes, it is."

"How's the computer?" Her father sauntered into the kitchen and leaned against the counter, crossing his arms.

"Better." She sighed. "I was having problems losing material I had typed into it but Reese . . . Mr. Edwards called someone and learned it was probably a power surge. We have a new device that should take care of it."

"Glad to hear it."

"What's a power surge?" Joel questioned from the kitchen doorway.

"I'll explain that later," Janet promised. "Come on, get your coat." They were going to Joel's favorite place, the Buffalo Bill Cody Memorial Museum. Janet had stopped counting the times she'd taken her brother to see the artifacts of the hunter's life. Afterward they stopped for hamburgers. Joel loved museums and Denver had several that fascinated the youth, especially the Buffalo Bill, the Firefighters' Museum and the Colorado Railroad Museum.

"Where do you want to go next week?" Janet asked as she let him off in front of her parents' home.

"The zoo," Joel replied without hesitation.

"I don't know; it may be closed by the time I get off work. We'll see, okay?"

A sad look rounded his eyes. "Okay, Janny, but try and get off early."

"I'll try," she promised.

Things looked good at the beginning of the week. Either the work load seemed lighter, or she was seeing the effects of having a computer. Janet was about to ask Reese if there was a possibility of her leaving a few hours early on Thursday, when he approached her.

"There's another computer class being offered this week. You seem comfortable with the

Simplex now, but I think it wouldn't be a bad idea for you to attend the class. I'll be happy to go along. There are several things I'd like to go over myself."

The offer took Janet by surprise. "I . . . I don't think I can. I'm booked up Thursdays."

"Every Thursday?" A dark brow was quirked mockingly.

"Yes," she responded crisply, not liking his attitude. "In fact, I was just about to ask if I could leave an hour early tomorrow."

Reese shrugged. "I don't see why not."

Janet came back from lunch Thursday afternoon and phoned her mother to say she'd be picking up Joel early. When she finished making the call she placed the headset over her ears to complete Reese's dictation before leaving. Another tape had been added to the stack and she knew she'd have to rush to get out of the office on time. As much as she hated to admit it, the computer worked wonderfully well and her fingers set a steady pace as they bounced over the keys.

A glance at her watch told her she'd finished with several minutes to spare. A brisk walk in the crisp autumn afternoon would be invigorating. Joel loved to toss the multicolored leaves in the air again and again. There wouldn't be many more afternoons they'd *be* able to enjoy being out of doors, since winter would be here shortly. She'd make sure today was special.

The door between the rooms was open and Janet smiled as she walked in to hand Reese the letters ready for his signature.

"I'm leaving now if there isn't anything else."

He didn't glance up. "As a matter of fact there is. I'll need this report as soon as possible."

A wary light crept into her bright blue eyes as she accepted the thick folder. Flipping through the handwritten pages, she estimated it would take several hours to complete.

Reese glanced up and leaned back in his chair.

The dismay was clearly etched in her features and she swallowed the objection.

"I wouldn't ask you, Janet, if it wasn't necessary." The quiet authority in his voice silenced the building anger.

"Of course," she murmured reluctantly. "I'll do this right away."

At her desk, Janet reviewed the material and heaved a sigh. There didn't seem to be anything in the report that looked that important. After pushing her glasses up on her nose with her index finger, she phoned her mother.

"Something's unexpectedly come up and I won't be able to make it after all," she told her, not bothering to disguise her own disappointment.

"Oh dear, maybe you'd better talk to Joel, you know how disappointed he's going to be. Wait a minute; I'll get him."

The line was silent until she heard her brother's

familiar voice. "Hi, Janny, I'm all ready. When will you get here?"

"Not until after the zoo closes, I'm afraid."

"But I wanted to go real bad. You said you were going to take me," he pleaded.

"I know, but there's nothing I can do. I have to stay late. Try and understand."

There was a long silence at the other end of the line, as if Joel was struggling within himself. "All right, Janny. I love you."

"I love you too. We'll talk later." Gently she replaced the receiver and glanced up to see Reese standing in the doorway between the two rooms. His face was twisted in a scowl, his blue eyes frigid cold and menacing.

"I don't pay you to make personal phone calls on my time. See that it doesn't happen again, Miss Montgomery."

Janet opened her mouth, then snapped it closed. She was so angry even her breathing was labored. Begin again? Her mind vaulted out Reese's words in accusation. Reese Edwards claimed he wanted to start again? Slowly Janet lowered her hands to her lap and prayed that God would help her control her temper.

By the time she had finished the prayer she felt better. She was still angry, but more in control of her reactions to that anger.

The report took three hours and it was almost seven before she placed it on Reese's desk. She was glad he wasn't there. He'd left the office without a word at six-thirty. No doubt he was meeting that "air head" blonde of his. Janet had watched him walk out of the room and her fingers had jammed the keys, causing mass confusion on the computer screen. Luckily it didn't take more than a minute to revise. For a second she didn't know if the reaction had been from the anger of doing this unnecessary report or the thought of him in Bunny Jacobs' arms.

The next morning there was a large floral arrangement waiting for Janet on her desk. She walked into the office and paused in midstep. Autumn-colored chrysanthemums in a beautifully designed ceramic vase. It was beautiful, her favorite flower. The attached card caught her attention and without taking off her coat she walked to her desk and removed the small white envelope. It read: THANKS FOR STAYING YESTERDAY. R.

"I see you found your present."

Her head shot up, bewilderment clouded her face. "Yes, it's not even Secretaries Day. Have you gotten your months confused?"

"Not at all." Both hands were in his pockets as he leaned indolently against the doorjamb. "I thought you deserved something extra for service above and beyond the call of duty."

Reese was apologizing the best way he could. Janet was shocked, but pleased. "I deserve something all right," she said with a bright smile, "two hours' overtime."

"You'll get that too." His voice was filled with humor. Their eyes met and the smile faded. "Peace, Janet."

She nodded, lowering her gaze. "Peace."

Samuel Edwards came into the office before lunch. "Good morning, Janet," he greeted her warmly. "Is that son of mine giving you gray hair?"

Her glasses were perched on the ridge of her nose and she twitched it in a futile attempt to place them where they belonged. "Not yet."

He chuckled to himself. "You certainly are a good looker."

Janet flushed. "Thank you, Mr. Edwards."

"Has that fool-headed boy asked you out yet?"

Uneasily Janet lowered her eyes, afraid her look would betray her feelings. "No, but I'm free Saturday night in case you're interested," she teased.

"Darned if I'm not," he chuckled. "Darned if I'm not."

Soon after his father's visit, Reese left for a meeting. "Janet, I can't find the Bressler file," he called with marked patience. "Will you see if you can locate it. I need it before noon."

It was a wonder he could locate anything at all with his desk a picture of chaos. Janet didn't know how anyone could head and maintain a company as involved and far-reaching as Dyna-Flow and have such poor organizational skills. Hands on hips, she stood staring at the stacks of files and correspondence that littered the desk and work area. There wasn't a single inch of space left uncluttered.

The first thing she did was to completely clear off the desk and organize everything into neat stacks. She located the missing file within minutes. Although his desk was usually a disaster, Janet knew that Reese kept everything systemized in his mind. It was only when he couldn't locate the actual item that he became frustrated and irrational. With a soft smile Janet placed the missing file along with phone messages in the center of his desk.

There was an accumulation of throwaway material she was about to dump in his trash can when she saw the picture. It was another of Reese's caricatures. Janet paused, withdrawing the paper from the wastepaper basket. It was one of Malcolm Hayes, the vice president, and so like him that Janet couldn't prevent a gentle smile. Reese was talented. Why he chose to throw his work away she didn't know.

It was obvious that he had sketched it during some kind of meeting. It was drawn on an ordinary piece of company stationery, and the quality of work was excellent. Janet took it and placed it in her desk drawer beside the one of

Reese's father she had discovered the year before.

Reese grabbed the file on his way out of the office later. "Thanks, Janet," he called. "I won't be back until four, and, Janet, darn"—he ran his fingers through his hair—"order flowers for Bunny. It's her birthday tomorrow."

Automatically Janet reached for the phone and tasted resentment. Would it always be like this when he asked her to do something for one of his blondes? She'd ordered flowers so many times in the past she didn't need to look up the phone number.

"Helen, this is Janet from Dyna-Flow. I'd like to order a dozen red roses from Mr. Edwards." Not only did she know the number, but she knew the girls who worked there. She should, she'd talked to them often enough.

"Oh, hi, Janet," Helen said, her voice slightly high. "Say, I finally met that boss of yours; he was in this morning. Practically pounded down the door."

"Mr. Edwards?"

"That's who he said he was. I put the bill on his account. One of the best-looking male specimens I've seen."

Janet sighed. "That's him. What was he doing at your place?" To her knowledge Reese had always left ordering flowers to her.

"He said he needed something extra special. I asked him about the roses—that's what you

73

normally order for him—but he shook his head. He must have spent fifteen minutes looking everything over. He said this girl would be offended if he sent her roses; what she deserved was orchids, but he didn't want to overwhelm her. He finally decided on my biggest display of chrysanthemums. Gorgeous fall colors. The vase alone is worth a small fortune."

Silly tears of happiness misted Janet's eyes as her gaze rested lovingly on the arrangement that dominated one side of her desk. Helen claimed Reese had said this girl deserved orchids; Janet loved orchids.

"Now who did you say I was supposed to send the roses to?" The voice effectively sliced into Janet's musings.

"Oh yes, the roses. Bunny Jacobs, Miss Bunny Jacobs."

Janet stared at the phone for a long time afterward. Get your head out of the clouds, Janet Montgomery, she told herself. It doesn't mean a thing, not a darn thing.

Gail came into the office at five and Janet was putting on her coat when Reese stormed into the room. He was more angry than Janet could remember seeing him in a long while.

His eyes spit fire from one girl to the other. "I'd like to speak to you in my office, Miss Montgomery. Now!"

Chapter Four

Reese was pacing the floor, his hands crossed over his chest, and for a moment Janet saw him as an Indian chief ready to wage battle.

"Yes?" Her voice was shaky.

"Is it true you're going out with my father Saturday night?" he lashed out, his voice heavy with contempt.

"What?" Janet asked, her eyes wide with shock.

A muscle twitched in his jaw. He leaned forward, placing the palms of his hands on the desk she'd recently cleared. "Just what kind of game are you playing anyway?"

"I'm not playing any games. I don't know what you're talking about," she denied.

If possible, his face hardened all the more. "Then what did my father mean when he said if I—" He paused and started again with controlled patience. "When he said he was taking you to dinner Saturday."

Mentally Janet reviewed the conversation with Samuel Edwards. "Oh," she inhaled, recalling the teasing.

"Is it or is it not true?" Reese demanded sharply.

"I don't believe that's any of your business, Mr. Edwards. My personal life is no concern of yours. I can date whom I please."

A vicious finger was directed at her. "I will not

tolerate my employees using my father for their own purposes. Is that understood?"

For a moment Janet stood frozen, unable to move. What kind of person did Reese think she was? "I understand all right," she mumbled. "I understand very well."

Pivoting sharply, she walked out of the door. She paused at her desk, dumped the flowers in the wastepaper basket and tucked the vase under her arm.

Gail looked shocked for a moment, then followed her out. "What was that all about?"

"You don't want to know." Her voice trembled with reaction.

"I may not want to know, but half the company heard what was going on he was shouting so loud. Are you really going out with the senior Mr. Edwards?"

"Of course not," Janet swallowed. "It was a joke, he didn't mean it any more than I did."

Gail shook her head and hurried her pace to match her friend's. "Teasing or not, Reese Edwards certainly took it seriously."

Hands on hips, Janet swiveled around. "Then that's his problem!"

The air hadn't cleared Monday morning and when Gail stopped by Janet's office on her way for coffee she whispered, "How can you two work together?"

"I do as I'm asked and nothing more. We don't

76

need to be bosom buddies for me to be his secretary."

"Yeah, but aren't you afraid of frostbite? I stepped in your office and the atmosphere was so cold I wanted to reach for a parka."

Janet took her coffee and sat at one of the long tables in the cafeteria. "I don't know what to do," she said with a long sigh. "He's leaving this afternoon and won't be back until late Thursday. Maybe everything will blow over by then."

"Have you tried praying about it?" Gail inquired gently.

"Oh honestly, Gail, of course I've tried. Well sort of, but it's hard."

"It's always difficult to pray for someone like Mr. Edwards, but Jesus claimed in the Sermon on the Mount that—"

"Now you're beginning to sound like my dad," Janet interrupted impatiently. "I grew up listening to a thousand sermons. I don't need one from my best friend."

Gail's hand cupped the Styrofoam cup. "I'm sorry. I didn't mean to sound preachy."

Janet swallowed uncomfortably. "I'm sorry too. I didn't need to be so rude. This thing is getting to me, more than I want to admit."

"It'd get to anyone."

Without a word to Janet, Reese walked out of the office before noon, his briefcase in his hand. For a moment Janet sat stunned.

He was leaving for the conference and hadn't left instructions for her or murmured one unnecessary word the entire morning. For one crazy minute she thought she was going to cry. How long could she continue to work with this cold war between them. Reese had been angry with her before, but nothing like this.

After lunch Janet discovered a curt list of instructions Reese had written for her on top of his desk. He hadn't even had the decency to hand it to her.

Janet was miserable all day. Gail was watching her closely on the way home, the dark eyes full of concern. Unusually quiet, Janet curled up on the sofa to read and wrapped a blanket over her feet. Gail and Ben were going out for a movie, and Janet was glad for the time alone. She felt the need for privacy tonight.

Gail wandered into the living room to wait for Ben. "What are you reading?"

Janet held up her Bible and smiled. "The Sermon on the Mount."

Gail chuckled and started to say something but was interrupted by Ben's knock. "I'll see you later; we can talk if you want."

Janet raised her hand and gave a friendly wave. "Have a good time."

She did pray for Reese, not so much for their relationship but for him as a man. She prayed for the conference he was attending, and his safety as he flew back to Denver. Her thoughts were dominated by him, and every time she felt depressed or worried she paused and murmured a quick prayer.

By Thursday afternoon Janet was eager to see him again. The thought surprised her as she placed the mail on his desk. He hadn't told her what time his flight landed; he'd only said when he would be in the office. Several times she found herself staring at the wall clock, mentally tabulating how much longer before he was due.

As it was he was twenty minutes late. Janet had long since run out of things to do and was cleaning out the filing cabinet when he opened the door to her office.

Her heart stopped at the sight of him. He looked tired, as if he hadn't slept the entire time he was away. Janet's hand froze on the file she was replacing. The tight line of his mouth told her he was in no better humor than when he'd left.

Her voice nearly failed her. "Welcome back, Mr. Edwards." Reese stopped and glared at her, his eyes dark and unfriendly.

Janet smiled, her lips trembling with the effort. She didn't know where the ability to greet him warmly had come from, but she didn't stop to question it. "I've placed the mail on your desk. There's a letter from Leon Fairfield you might wish to read over, but other than that everything has run smoothly while you were away." Her lashes fluttered downward as the ability to meet his eyes deserted her. She finished placing the folder in the filing cabinet.

"It's good to be back."

Somehow Janet had expected a sarcastic reply or a bitter retort, but not friendliness or relief in his voice. Slowly, very slowly she raised her eyes to meet his. Reese was smiling. One of those earth-shattering, bone-melting smiles he was capable of delivering without the least effort. There wasn't a woman alive who wouldn't be affected by it. Relief washed over Janet, and for the first time in days she relaxed.

Reese entered his office and fifteen minutes later buzzed for her. Janet knew him well enough to realize he'd want to deal with his mail first, so she took her steno pad and pencil in with her.

She wasn't halfway through the door when he ordered, "Take a letter." Automatically she sat in the chair opposite his desk, her mouth curved upward. Things were back to normal.

Partway through typing up Reese's correspondence, she was buzzed by him again. "Can you stay late tonight, Janet? There's an estimate I'd like to have completed for Tom Wilson." Her hesitation was only momentary, but enough for Reese to notice. "I forgot," he said with dry sarcasm, "it's Thursday. Forget I asked."

"How . . . how late?" She didn't want to do

anything to destroy this fragile cease-fire between them.

He hesitated. "About an hour, maybe two."

"I'll stay, if I can use the phone for a personal call."

She could hear amusement in his voice. "Feel free."

As soon as she released the button for the intercom, Janet phoned her mother.

"I have to stay late tonight," she explained.

"Oh dear. Joel's going to be disappointed. This happened last week too." Her mother sighed.

"I know. Is there any possibility you can bring him to the office." Janet hated to ask, especially since her mother didn't like driving in the downtown traffic. But she hated to disappoint her brother two consecutive weeks. "We were going to a movie and still could if I didn't need to pick him up."

"What a good idea." There was a quick rush of noise from the background, probably from Joel. "What time should I be there?"

Janet gave her mother the time and buzzed Reese. "Everything's been arranged, Mr. Edwards. Joel's meeting me here."

"Fine." The one word was clipped and controlled. "Get Bunny Jacobs on the phone for me; I have some arrangements of my own to make." Janet pressed her lips together so tightly her teeth hurt.

When Janet had the correspondence ready for Reese's signature, he handed her several pages of the detailed estimate. A quick review showed that it wasn't as complicated as she expected and she would probably have it done in the time allotted.

Her mother and Joel walked in while the report was coming out of the printer.

"Hi, Janny." Joel looked around the room with curious eyes. "What's that?" He pointed to the intercom on her desk.

"It's called an intercom. I use it to talk to my boss, Mr. Edwards," she explained. "Be sure and don't touch it."

"Will it be all right to leave now?" her mother quizzed, glancing around the unfamiliar surroundings. "Your father's double-parked and I don't want to be long."

"Sure. Go ahead, Mom. And thanks." Janet walked her mother to the door and turned to see Joel press down the switch to the intercom.

"Joel," she snapped. "I told you to leave that alone."

"Oh heavens. I hope you're going to be finished here soon," her mother sighed. "Otherwise Joel's going to be a handful."

"We'll manage."

No sooner had the door closed after her mother than Reese stepped out of his office. Janet's nerves jumped at the harsh amusement in his face.

"What's going on here? I was on the phone

and . . ." He stopped, noticing Joel for the first time.

As always when someone first met her brother, Janet experienced a defensive rush of emotion. One look told even the casual observer that her brother was different, and often the response was less than kind.

"Joel, you must apologize to Mr. Edwards for playing with the intercom," she said sternly.

Joel hung his head. It was rare that Janet used that tone of voice with him and she moved behind him, placing a gentle hand on his shoulder. She hoped the contact would lessen the sharpness in her voice.

"I'm sorry." He slurred the words, as he often did when chastised.

"This is Joel?" Surprise flickered briefly over the handsome features.

Janet tensed. Had the look on Reese's face been revulsion?

"Joel's your Thursday night date?"

Janet nodded. "Joel, this is my boss, Mr. Edwards."

Reese stepped forward and held out his hand to the youth. "I'm pleased to meet you."

Joel looked up, his boyish face alight with a wide grin as he accepted the hand and shook it vigorously. "Janny works for you?"

"Yes, Janny does." Reese's eyes met Janet's, whose were wary and uncertain.

"We're going to a movie," Joel explained enthusiastically. "We go to lots of movies. We were supposed to go to the zoo last week but Janny had to work." His face saddened. "But she took me Saturday."

Reese's head shot up, his gaze narrowed. "It was my understanding you were seeing my father Saturday."

Janet was grateful that her brother was standing in front of her and she could support her hands on his shoulders. "I told you he'd only been teasing."

The dark eyes hardened. "That old coot." The words were expelled in an angry rush.

"What's a coot?" Joel asked innocently.

"A weak-minded old man," Reese explained as he smoothed the hair along the side of his head in an agitated movement.

The printer had stopped and Janet moved behind it to collect the printed estimate. "I'll have this for you in a minute."

"That's fine. Want to see my office, Joel?" Reese invited, holding the door open for the youth.

Joel's eyes rounded with excitement. "Sure. Can I push buttons?"

"We'll see."

Janet stood back, her expression tight and worried. Of all the people in the world she would never have expected Reese Edwards to accept her brother so easily. He liked perfection; one look at the women he dated said as much.

Working as quickly as possible, Janet compiled the estimate in a neat pile. She was uncomfortable leaving Joel with Reese for too long. Too many things could go wrong.

She stepped into his office and set the report on the edge of the desk. Joel was sitting in Reese's high-backed leather chair, leaning as far back as the seat would extend, his feet propped on the corner of the desk. A smile came automatically. "Honestly, Joel, you look more pleased than Boss Hogg at feeding time."

Reese's deep-throated chuckle caused Janet to glance away. "Is that what you think when I sit like, that?" he questioned, his eyes glowing with a mischievous grin.

Janet locked her hands in front of her. Reese loved to fluster her. "I didn't mean to imply," she began shakily, "but—"

"If the shoe fits," he finished for her.

"Exactly."

"You know"—Reese leaned against the chair situated opposite Joel, crossing his outstretched legs in front of Janet—"it's been years since I went to a movie."

"Wanna come?" Joel was so eager that he knocked a stack of files onto the floor as he swung his feet down.

Tight-lipped, Janet knelt to pick up the pile. Reese met her on the carpet as he stooped down to help her.

"I'm sure Mr. Edwards is too busy to come with us tonight, Joel. Maybe another time." She scrambled to replace the documents on his desk.

"I'm not busy," Reese contradicted. "And I'll buy the popcorn."

Joel's eyes immediately lit up enthusiastically.

"But you must be exhausted." She paused to study his expression, hoping to read the real reason for his sudden desire to be with them.

"Not at all."

Nervously Janet moistened her lips. "Then of course you're welcome." The invitation lacked welcome and was issued almost grudgingly. Janet didn't know why he was doing this. And she wasn't sure she approved.

Not that she had reason to fault him. Reese was wonderful with Joel. In the past Janet had noted that people, especially those who hadn't been around Joel, tended to talk down to him, or relate to him on a childish level. It amazed Janet that Reese could act so naturally with her brother. He teased and laughed with Joel as if they were longtime friends.

"I like Mr. Reese," Joel stated from the backseat of the car on the way home. He sat on the edge of the cushion, leaning as far forward into the front seat as the car would allow.

Janet sighed. Joel had a habit of talking about people as if they weren't there. "Mr. Edwards can be a very nice person," she agreed.

86

"Can be?" Reese murmured the question for her ears alone. His eyes flickered off the road to glance at her. The searing look sent her pulse racing.

"But he makes you work late sometimes and then you can't take me places," Joel continued.

"If I promise not to do that, will you let me come with you again? Thursday nights can be boring without someone special."

Janet wanted to scream at Reese. What did he mean someone special? He was using her brother to get to her. What possible interest could he have in entertaining Joel? Clenching her hands into a white-knuckled fist, Janet glared at Reese.

"There's always Bunny," she whispered in a waspish tone.

"True, there's always Bunny," he returned, his smile stilted and polite.

"I want Mr. Reese to come with us. He buys me popcorn."

Janet bit into her lip to keep from saying that Mr. Edwards was accustomed to paying for his "friends." Turning her face to look out the side window, Janet pretended to be interested in the downtown lights. She had become so catty lately, almost spiteful. It was unlike her and she hated these thoughts that hounded her. Strangely, they always centered around Reese and Bunny. Could it possibly be that she was jealous?

"Ha!" She laughed. Bunny Jacobs could have him for all she cared.

"Pardon?" Reese gave her a funny look. "Did you say something?"

"No," she said uneasily. "I didn't say a thing."

When they'd left the office for the theater, Reese had insisted on driving. Janet couldn't put up much of an argument when a blissful Joel was unable to tear his look from the plush vehicle. Now she regretted not having her own car.

After the movie Reese had asked Joel his address, which her brother had proudly repeated. It was obvious from the route he was driving that Reese intended to drop off Joel first. When he did, Janet would insist on staying. Her father could take her home later and she'd pick up her car tomorrow after work. Everything was decided logically in her mind. The less time she spent with Reese the better.

"That's it." Joel pointed out his house for Reese, who pulled alongside of the curb and parked the car.

In a flash Joel jumped out of the seat and ran for the front door.

Janet sighed irritably. "No doubt he wants to show my dad your car." Her guess couldn't have been more correct. Even before Janet could climb from the front seat, her father, mother and Joel were coming out of the house.

Reese got out of the car and stood beside Janet.

"Mom and Dad, I'd like you to meet Mr. Edwards, the president of Dyna-Flow."

"And he bought me popcorn and orange drink and these chewy candies and let me ride in his car. And he says he wants to go again with Janet and me and . . ." Joel paused, taking in a giant breath.

"I think we get the idea, Joel," Stewart Montgomery admonished gently, extending his hand to Reese. "I've heard a lot about you, Mr. Edwards. It's a pleasure to meet you at last."

"The pleasure's mine, Ms. Montgomery." His head dipped slightly as he directed his look to her mother. "Now I understand where Janet gets those beautiful blue eyes."

"Why, thank you." Leonora smiled, genuinely pleased, her round face flushed with the compliment.

Janet's fists knotted at her side. She would have loved to quietly inform Reese Edwards that her eyes were brown, but unfortunately he was right. She half expected him to claim that she and her mother must be sisters. It sounded like a line he'd use.

"Perhaps you'd like to come in for coffee?" Janet heard her mother's invitation and her mouth tightened. She didn't want Reese to involve himself further in her life.

"Yes, I would, but only if you call me Reese. I get enough of the 'Mr. Edwards' at the office." The dig, however slight, hit its mark.

"Would you prefer it if I called you Bunnytoes?"

she hissed under her breath as she followed her parents into the house.

The hand guiding her elbow squeezed her arm. "No, I wouldn't," he murmured, the anger in his low voice barely controlled. "You don't want me here, do you?"

"No," she snapped, knowing she was being unreasonable. She didn't care. How could they maintain an impersonal, professional relationship if he was making friends with Joel and spending time with her parents?

He halted at the screen door. The front door was open, for Janet and Reese to come inside. Janet could see her mother busy in the kitchen, and her father was helping Joel with something.

Color flowed quickly into her face and she was painfully aware of her rude and senseless behavior.

"Come in, you two," her father called, his eyes silently questioning Janet.

Reese hesitated for only a moment before raising his hand and pushing open the screen. Janet preceded him inside. The shag carpet was worn and the furniture outdated and threadbare. Funny, she hadn't noticed these things before, but she was seeing the room with new eyes, just as Reese must be seeing it. Straightening her back in a gesture of pride, Janet walked into the kitchen to help her mother.

Leonora was busy taking bread and sliced meat

from the refrigerator, "I imagine you didn't have time for dinner."

"Mom," Janet protested. "Don't do this. You don't need to impress Mr. Edwards."

Her mother straightened, wiping her hands on the terry-cloth apron. "It's no trouble, dear; you know that."

Janet knew her mother well enough to realize it was useless to argue. Her mother's ability to make people feel comfortable and wanted had often impressed Janet. Now it embarrassed her.

Janet brought out the coffee while Reese and her father sat deep in conversation. Joel was perched on a footstool at Reese's feet. That irritated her all the more. Reese Edwards had adoring women at his feet all the time; it angered Janet to see one of her family there.

Janet sat on the other side of the room, as far away from Reese as possible. He cast her a quick look and the edge of his mouth curled up in an expression of contempt and amusement, as if he were aware of exactly what she was doing.

"School tomorrow, Joel," Leonora reminded him.

"Ah, Mom."

"Joel." One word from his father was enough to silence any protest.

Anxious to remove herself as quickly as possible from the uncomfortable situation, Janet leaped to her feet. "I'll help."

"No need, Janet; the boy can help himself," her

91

father said gently, but again his gaze searched hers. The faded blue eyes narrowed slightly, as if he read something there and disapproved.

Slowly Janet sat down, feeling almost numb. Who would have believed she could feel so disconcerted and out of place in her own family home?

"I really should be going," Reese insisted as he stood. "Thank you for the sandwich, Mrs. Montgomery." He handed her the empty plate. Janet hadn't touched hers. "I'm pleased to have met you both. Don't worry about Janet. I'll see her safely to her car and follow her home."

Janet was just about to ardently protest when her father thanked him and the two men walked out the door.

"What is the matter with you tonight?" her mother demanded. "You're jumpier than water on a hot griddle."

Janet's throat constricted painfully. "I'm sorry, Mom."

"It's not me who requires an apology," she said with a sternness that surprised Janet. It wasn't enough that Reese Edwards was forcing himself into her home and into her life. Now her own mother was speaking to her as if she were a disobedient child.

Reese was already waiting for her in the Mercedes. Her father held open the passenger door and shut it for her once she was inside.

Her shaking hands snapped the seat belt into place. If the atmosphere was strained inside the house, it was nothing compared to the open hostility that existed in the small enclosure of the car.

Reese rounded a corner with unnecessary speed, the tires squealed and Janet released a shuddering breath. "Please don't," she pleaded in a weak voice.

"Don't what?" he demanded.

"Speed."

"I thought you were eager to remove yourself from my undesirable presence." He slammed on the brakes to avoid running a red light. Janet was thrown forward until the seat belt locked, preventing her from hitting the dashboard.

"I'm not that eager."

He stared straight ahead, waiting for the light to change. "You could have fooled me."

"Reese, please."

He expelled his breath impatiently. "Reese," he mimicked, his voice ragged with irritation. "What happened to the polite and formal 'Mr. Edwards'?"

"I called you Mr. Edwards for two years. Why should it make a difference now?" she shouted, fighting the waves of misery that threatened to drown her.

Dark fires flashed from his eyes and Janet witnessed the tight control he had on his emotions. "Because it does." He breathed in heavily, his hand gripping the steering wheel until the knuckles turned pale.

"You . . . you think that because I let you kiss me I should be so overwhelmed by your charm that I'll crumble at your feet? Is that it? If you hadn't noticed, I'm not Bunny or any other of your blonde bombshells. Use your techniques on them, and leave me alone."

He shot her a threatening look. "You don't need to remind me who you are. At least Bunny has a warm heart. A man could get frostbite sitting beside you!"

Janet sucked in her breath at the sharp pain that seemed to reach out and physically slap her. To her horror, tears welled in her eyes, threatening to crash over the thick wall of her lashes. Averting her face, she glared out the side window, her composure shredding thread by thread until she felt naked and vulnerable.

The light changed and Reese sped ahead as if he couldn't be rid of her fast enough. The silence between them seemed to crackle and spark like an electrical storm. When he pulled off the street into the parking lot reserved for company employees, her hand was braced against the door handle. One hot tear slid down her face, followed by another and another. In a desperate effort to abate their fall, Janet held her breath.

The Mercedes had no sooner pulled to a stop in

94

front of her car than Janet jumped out. Without a backward glance she slammed the door. Reese's car made a screeching noise as it pulled out of the parking lot.

With hands that were trembling so badly she could barely insert the key into the slot, Janet opened the car and scooted inside. Suddenly it all became too much and her shoulders heaved in giant sobs. Confused, unsure and miserable, she buried her face in her hands. It had been years since she had cried like this, as if she'd lost the most precious, the most wonderful thing in her life.

What had been the turning point tonight? Where had things gone wrong? After he'd kissed her that night she'd tried so desperately to place their relationship on an even keel. With that same kind of urgency she had struggled to confine Reese to the area of her life that involved the office. It had been useless. How could she when thoughts of him dominated every waking minute? She'd prayed so hard, tried so hard.

Suddenly her door was wrenched open and Janet gave a startled gasp as Reese hauled her out of the car. Her feet weren't allowed to touch the street as his arms wrapped themselves around her, lifting her until their eyes met, hers red and puffy, his dark and tormented.

With a small joyous cry she wrapped her arms around his neck and brought his mouth to hers.

Crushed against him so hard she could hardly breathe, Janet clung with every fiber of strength she possessed.

Their mouths ravaged one another, slanting across each other's, twisting, bruising, demanding, giving, surrendering.

A hand on either side of her face, Reese pulled back and gently rubbed his thumb over her lips. "You've been driving me crazy all week," he whispered, and just the way he said it was all the convincing she'd ever need that it was true. His eyes searched hers.

As she stood before him in the light of the moon, a quivering smile formed and she stood on tiptoes to brush her lips over his. All these strange wonderful feelings were shining from her eyes. It was there; she recognized it instantly. The feeling that had been missing with Gary, that depth of emotion, desire, need. If Reese was cruel to her now, she'd die.

"Don't look at me like that," Reese demanded suddenly, his voice gruff. He cradled her in his arms, brushing the hair away from her face so he could whisper intimately in her ear. "Come home with me, Janet, spend the night."

Chapter Five

As the shock of his words washed over her, Janet knew what it must feel like to die. She was unbelievably calm, almost numb.

Reese frowned, watching the expression on her face.

His gaze was hypnotic and Janet couldn't force her eyes away. "I'm not one of your blondes."

Reese closed his eyes and opened them again before inhaling a sharp breath. "I thought we'd already determined that. Janet, listen." Hands cupping her face, he brought her lips to his with an infinite gentleness, kissing her tenderly, threatening to overwhelm her. "I've wanted you for weeks," he whispered, his voice ragged. "Can't you see you're driving me crazy?"

Hands on his chest, Janet could feel the powerful beat of his heart against the palms of her hands.

"You want me too, don't deny it."

She couldn't. It was true. "Yes, I . . . I want you, but I can't. I can't." She wrenched herself out of his embrace and backed away, her arms cradling her middle. Reese didn't know what it was to truly love someone. He didn't want commitment. She had watched him for two years, had witnessed the progression of women in and out of his life. The pattern was always the same. He'd wait until his latest blonde would show signs of falling in love with him, then sever the relationship. Reese didn't want love, he wanted . . . the word refused to form in her mind.

"Why not?" He didn't attempt to bring her back into his arms. "If you want me and I want you then what's there to stop us? You're over twenty-one. We can keep this relationship confidential and out of the office."

"That's not it." She took another step backward because he was beginning to make sense. Because she realized how much she desired him. "I . . . I've been raised with high moral values I . . ." She paused and dropped her hands, forming tight fists of resolve. "I just can't. I'd hate myself in the morning. What seems so right tonight would be sordid and ugly when we wake up."

"It wouldn't," Reese argued. "You'll wake in my arms and I'll kiss away any doubts."

"Reese, no." Her voice was shaking. "Please accept that. I can't, I just can't."

His dark head nodded, his blue eyes clear. "All right, I agree. Maybe it is too soon. We'll give it time, test this thing."

Janet was more unsure than ever. How could they possibly maintain a working relationship with a strong sexual current running between them?

He opened her car door for her, but before she could climb inside he took her into his arms and gently kissed her. It was sweet and beautiful, and Janet felt herself transcended, reaching heights of awareness she had never known existed. If he had been rough or demanding, Janet wouldn't have had any difficulty pushing him away. But this infinite tenderness weakened her.

She lay awake for a long time analyzing her feelings. Was she in love with Reese Edwards? Her mind didn't seem to have an answer. She was strongly attracted to him, more than she had ever been to any man. But she couldn't confuse physical attraction with love.

Janet was grateful it was Friday when she woke with the alarm early the next morning. Glad, but not for the normal reasons. She dressed carefully, fearing that whatever she chose would be read as some unspoken invitation.

As was his habit, Reese was already in his office when she arrived. The door between their rooms was open.

After the coffee had finished brewing she took a cup in to him and set it on the corner of his desk. "Good morning," she said crisply.

"Good morning, Janet." He replied in the same businesslike tone, but when he raised his eyes to her he was smiling.

"Did you sleep well?"

"Wonderfully." Liar, liar, her mind accused. "And you?"

"Restless, very restless." The corners of his

mouth quivered with the effort of suppressing a smile.

"I'm sorry to hear that." She strived to sound aloof and uncaring.

"Not sorry enough," he murmured under his breath, and Janet inhaled sharply. Her back rigid she removed a stack of files from the out-basket and turned.

"Janet," he called her and when she swung around he winked. "Relax, will you?"

Releasing the breath she'd unconsciously been holding, she nodded. "Yes, Mr. Edwards."

The morning passed pleasantly, much to Janet's surprise. She felt as though she'd been walking on eggshells for so long that any release in the terrible tension was bound to help.

Gail noted Janet's renewed appetite at lunch. "Do you actually mean you're going to order something more than the soup du jour? My ears must be deceiving me. Food, solid food."

"Oh, Gail, cut it out," Janet said and laughed. "You seem pretty chipper yourself. Something good must be happening."

Gail arched both finely shaped brows and grinned. Janet regarded her closely. "All right, Gail Templeton, you look like a Cheshire cat grinning at me. Something's happened and you're bursting to tell me."

Her dark eyes sparkled as Gail scooted closer to the table. "Well, actually I guess you could say something wonderful's happened. Ben asked me to marry him last night." Her own happiness at the news was reflected on her face.

"Congratulations! Not that I'm surprised. You've been seeing a lot of one another lately."

"We haven't got the rings yet, so don't say anything. Ben wants to talk to my parents first. I know they'll approve; Mom and Dad have always liked Ben. I'm so lucky, Janet. There isn't anyone in the world I'd rather have than Ben, I love him so much."

"How'd you know you were in love with him?" Janet's fingers curled around the water glass. It sounded like an unusual question and she felt uneasy. "I mean, when did you realize what you felt for Ben was love?"

Gail sighed and her shoulders slouched forward slightly. "I'm not exactly sure when. It's not like I could put an actual date on it. Ben and I had been dating now and then. Sort of the way you and Gary have in the past. I liked him, but he wasn't special."

"What changed?"

Gail shrugged and swept the palm of her hand in front of her. "I'm not really sure. I liked Ben as a friend and gradually that friendship matured into love. You might say it caught on fire because we've been seeing each other almost every night for weeks now."

"I know," Janet teased.

"After we talk to my parents, we're going to ask your father if he'll marry us."

"Dad would be honored." Janet recalled her father's mentioning several months before that he wouldn't be surprised if Gail and Ben decided to marry. Janet hadn't thought much of the comment. Yet he'd known even before they did.

Malcolm Hayes was in Reese's office when Janet returned from lunch, and the connecting door was closed.

The phone rang and Janet picked up the receiver. "Mr. Edwards' office."

"Hello, Miss Montgomery, this is Bunny, Can I speak to Reese?"

The familiar sugar-coated voice sent chills straight up Janet's spine. "I'm sorry, Bunny, but Mr. Edwards is in a meeting. Can I take a message?"

"Tell him I called. And, Miss Montgomery, please tell him its very, very important."

Janet's pen flew across the pink memo pad. "I'll do that." Replacing the receiver a moment later, she underlined the large capital letters: <u>VERY, VERY IMPORTANT.</u>

The call troubled her most of the afternoon. She should be grateful, she chided herself angrily as she replaced a file. Bunny Jacobs' call helped her put things into perspective. She wasn't one of Reese's empty-headed females. She had brains, brains enough to know there was nothing but heartache ahead if she allowed herself to become entangled by his charms.

Other than the necessary office dialogue, Janet didn't speak to Reese for the remainder of the afternoon. She cleared her desk at quitting time and was waiting for Gail when Reese moved into the front of the office.

"Have a nice weekend, Janet." His deep blue eyes did a lazy appraisal of her.

"Thank you," she murmured nervously. "I will." Janet relaxed when Reese returned to his office. What had she expected? Did she think he was going to suggest a date for the weekend? She should be grateful he hadn't. Yet a nagging sense of disappointment came over her. What did it matter? Janet asked herself. She had long ago decided to say no to any suggestion he offered.

Gail and Ben were going to Gail's parents' home for dinner, and Janet was left to her own devices for the evening. Reading over the menu, she noted a movie that looked interesting and popped a frozen pizza in the oven. She hated to cook, and Gail was much better at it.

Fifteen minutes later the timer dinged and Janet pulled out the cookie sheet. She had no sooner set it on top of the counter than the doorbell chimed. Wiping her hands on her apron, she walked across the room and looked through the peephole. Reese. She closed her eyes a moment and expelled a long, shuddering breath before opening the door.

"What are you doing here?" she asked, her breath fast and uneven. She was accustomed to seeing Reese in business suits, and now he was dressed casually in dark slacks and a burgundy pullover sweater. One look at the compelling male figure and Janet knew she was fighting a losing battle. She wouldn't be honest if she refused to admit she was pleased to see him.

"I've come to see you," he said, and the grooves around his mouth deepened into a smile. "Have you eaten?"

Her poise cracking, Janet gestured toward the kitchen. "I . . . I was just about to have something. You're welcome to share a bite if you'd like."

"Oh, I'd like all right," he mumbled, but his gaze was centered on her mouth.

Nervously Janet moistened her lips with her tongue and with a muted groan Reese pulled her into his arms.

Calling herself every kind of fool, Janet wrapped her arms around his neck without restraint. Their mouths strained against one another as if they couldn't give, couldn't receive enough.

Janet's legs were no steadier than the autumn leaves falling to the earth in the world outside her door.

Reese kissed her again and again, parting her mouth, his lips a seductive weapon.

"No." She pulled away and buried her face in

his sweater. Her eager and immediate response to his touch rippled over her like shock waves. "No," she repeated with less conviction.

Reese's hands were in her hair, extracting the pins that held it neatly in place and tossing them carelessly aside as his fingers weaved through the chestnut-colored length.

As soon as her hair was free, Janet could feel Reese's breath stirring the hair at the top of her head as if drinking in the fresh fragrance.

"Your lips are saying no." The voice was low and rasping as he pulled away slightly to study her. "But I'm getting very different signals from your body." His lips brushed a kiss against the sensitive skin at the hollow of her throat. "Did anyone ever tell you, you had a passionate mouth?"

Janet squeezed her eyes shut and jerked herself free. Passionate mouth indeed. No doubt that was another line he tossed out to every one of his blondes.

"Please." She backed up, extending her arms out in front of her to keep him away. "Why are you here?"

Reese was silently laughing at her, his amusement causing crinkling crow's-feet at his eyes. "I came to take you to dinner." He took a step toward her. "I didn't say anything at the office this afternoon because you would have said no."

Janet's head snapped up and her eyes widened. Could Reese read her thoughts as well?

It wouldn't do any good to argue with him. Reese Edwards wouldn't accept it from her.

"But the pizza . . ." She gestured weakly toward the kitchen.

"Save it for your lunch tomorrow. Now go change, something casual."

Janet could almost hate him for the high-handed, authoritarian attitude, but she knew exchanging words would be useless.

She took her time deciding what to wear, finally choosing a soft pair of jeans and a light pink sweater.

Reese was sitting on the sofa, leafing through some religious magazines her father had given her. He stood when he saw her, his face looking puzzled. "Are these yours?" he questioned as he glanced over at her sharply.

A gentle smile lifted the corners of her mouth. "No, they belong to my dad. He's letting me read them."

Reese turned over the magazine and Janet watched as the color seemed to wash out of his face. "Your father is a pastor?"

"Minister, pastor, man of God. Yes."

Reese sat down and the sofa dipped as it accepted his weight. "And is his daughter a—"

"A woman of God?" She finished the question for him.

Reese nodded.

"Yes, I am."

Janet watched as Reese breathed in deeply, as if to gain control of himself. "Why didn't you say something last night? You must think me a heel."

"No more than usual," she replied with a crooked smile.

Reese's gaze locked with hers. "I always knew there was something different about you. No," he corrected himself, "not different, special."

A rush of pleasure cast her gaze downward. She picked an imaginary piece of lint off her jeans. "Thank you," she said and moved across the room to withdraw a jacket from the closet.

"Is there anyplace special you'd like to eat?" Reese asked as he tucked a guiding hand beneath her elbow.

"After all those Thursday night outings with Joel, I'd settle for anyplace that doesn't serve hamburgers."

Reese opened the car door for her and came around to the other side of the car to climb into the driver's seat. "After dinner I thought we might catch a movie at the International Film Festival."

"I'd like that."

They ate enchiladas in a Mexican restaurant that had atmosphere and wonderful food. Reese teasingly insisted on large pieces of apple pie for desert. Their conversation was friendly and relaxed, as if they were old friends. It surprised

Janet that they could act so naturally with each other. Only a few days earlier it had seemed an impossibility. Janet had always had respect and admiration for Reese, but she had never really known him as a person. It didn't take her long to decide she appreciated his wit and sense of humor.

There were several films showing, and Janet was pleased when Reese suggested the French film. They were standing in line outside the theater when Reese asked, "If you don't mind subtitles."

"I speak French," she announced casually. "My parents were missionaries in Guadeloupe, a small French island in the Caribbean. I was born there. Until I was five I spoke better French than English."

Reese glanced down at her, his mouth quirked upward. "You're full of surprises, aren't you? Are you fluent in any other languages?"

"I speak a smidgen of Spanish. At least enough to get me through two summers working with missionaries building a church in central Mexico."

Their hands were entwined and Janet enjoyed the sensation of being tied to Reese, even if it was only for the moment.

"Did you consider becoming a missionary?" His gaze narrowed fractionally.

"Never," she denied vehemently. "I was in Mexico the summers between my junior and senior years in high school. My intentions were terrible. The only reason I went was to get away from my parents. I was angry with them and with God."

"Why?"

She shrugged, not wishing to go into the details. "It's a long story."

Reese's hand pushed back a stray curl that the wind had whipped across Janet's face. His touch lingered longer than necessary. "I can't picture you as a rebellious teenager."

Janet's laugh was short, almost sharp. "I was that and more. My mother claims I gave her every white hair she has."

"But her hair's completely white."

Janet's sigh was full of amusement. "See what I mean?"

His chuckle was low and pleasant-sounding. Dropping her hand, he tucked his arm around her waist and drew her close to his side. "I'll have you know I was a model child," he informed her. "I never gave my parents a moment's worry. While other kids were into drugs, booze and wild parties, I stayed home and studied."

For a second Janet was sure he was teasing, but one look at the sincerity in his face and she couldn't doubt the truth. "You're making up for lost time now, is that it?"

His mouth moved into a mocking line. "I guess you could say that."

Reese paid for their tickets and they moved into the theater. "Before we sit down, do you want any popcorn?"

Janet looked at him, feigning shock. "You don't eat popcorn during a French film. This is serious stuff."

Reese moved slowly to stand over her, shaking his head. "Do you want popcorn or not?"

"No, thanks."

The film was excellent and they discussed the plot and theme all the way back to her apartment. Reese parked in front of the building and they sat in the car discussing the film for another ten minutes.

"Do you want to come in?" Janet asked. "I can make some coffee, or cocoa, whatever you like."

"Whatever I like?" he repeated mockingly. "I doubt that." His look was full of suggestion and Janet's stomach muscles tightened. His hand reached out to caress the smooth cheek and gradually moved around the back of her neck, drawing her face to his.

Her resolve to make this a lighthearted time began to melt away, bit by bit, drop by drop as their lips drew closer and closer.

The pressure stopped when only a fraction of an inch separated their mouths. Reese's eyes darkened as they studied first her face and then her moist lips.

Unable to endure the sweet, tantalizing torture, Janet lowered her eyelids, afraid he could read what was there.

With a moan, his mouth settled over hers. Again he was gentle, so gentle. Her submission to him was complete as he wrapped his arms around her, bringing her as close as humanly possible. The kiss deepened with demanding hunger, and Janet responded with an eagerness she couldn't disguise.

When the kiss ended, their breathing was labored, almost ragged. Arms wrapped around his neck, Janet gently laid her head on his shoulder. "Is this real?" She was surprised to hear herself, unaware she had voiced the question.

"If it isn't, I don't want to wake up, unless it's with you in my arms."

Reason was forsaken, banished, gone. If he made the same invitation tonight, Janet didn't know if she had the will to resist. She didn't know if this feeling for Reese was love, but it ran deep, intense, frightening and wonderful.

He kissed her again, but didn't allow the passion to deepen. "I won't accept your invitation to come in, but not because I don't want to." His voice was low-pitched and his gaze swept her face, his eyes dark and vibrant.

Janet nodded. She closed her eyes, telling Reese she understood and was grateful. He escorted her to the apartment door, kissing her again.

A half hour later Janet sat on top of her bed, her velour housecoat wrapped around her feet as she waited for Gail. This feeling, this thing that was happening with Reese was too wonderful to keep to herself any longer. A gentle smile curved up the ends of her mouth. Gail would be shocked. So would anyone from Dyna-Flow. Until now their relationship had been strictly business.

The phone rang and Janet flinched with surprise. Who would be phoning this late? Joel. Something had happened to Joel. She flew off the bed and raced into the living room, jerking the phone off the hook.

"Yes?" she breathed.

"Janet?" It was Reese.

"Reese?" she said and expelled her breath forcefully. "You scared the living daylights out of me. I thought it must be my parents and something had happened to Joel."

"I apologize. I didn't mean to frighten you."

Her heart had returned to a normal pace and she sank into the sofa, curling her bare feet beneath her. "That's all right. I'd rather talk to you."

"Were you asleep?"

"No, not yet."

"I want to see you tomorrow. I realized when I got home that I hadn't said anything. There's someplace I want to take you, show you."

Just the way he said it, the inflection in his voice, the husky intonation told Janet this "someplace" was special. "I'd like that, I'd like it very much."

"It's in the mountains," he hesitated. "We'll be alone all day." Again he paused. "It might be a good idea if someone else came along."

"Joel?" Janet knew what Reese was saying and appreciated the thoughtfulness. He was having trouble keeping his hands off her. What he didn't know was how much trouble she was having not touching him.

"Joel would enjoy the trip," Reese murmured. "Is ten too early?"

Five minutes later Janet hung up the phone. She sat for another fifteen, drinking in the conversation, playing back every word in her mind.

Dressed in jeans and a sweatshirt, Janet was ready and waiting by the time Reese arrived. Her dad had brought Joel over, and her mother had sent along freshly baked cookies. Janet had packed a small lunch, including cold pizza from the night before, and added the cookies to the basket.

"Where are we going, Janny?" Joel asked her for the tenth time in as many minutes.

"I don't know. Reese didn't tell me."

"I like Mr. Reese, I like him a lot."

Janet placed her arm across her brother's shoulders. "I do too."

Gail sauntered into the living room. "I only hope

you know what you're doing. Be careful," she reminded her friend, and she wasn't speaking about hiking or camping. They had sat up for a long time talking after Gail arrived home last night. Janet had been surprised at her friend's reaction. She'd expected Gail to be happy for her, pleased. Instead Gail had been wary, unsure. "You know what Reese Edwards is like with women."

"Of course I do," Janet stated calmly. "But it's different with me. I know it is."

"Don't you think every woman he dates tells herself that?"

The logic of her question had raised doubts, but they had quickly been dispelled. She wasn't like his other women, it had to be different this time. It must be.

Reese arrived at precisely ten, allowing Joel to carry down the picnic basket. His greeting to Gail was polite, almost stilted, and for a fleeting second Janet had the impression he was sorry someone from the office had seen them together. But the thought passed quickly.

"Where are we going?" Joel asked again, but this time from the backseat of the moving car.

"Yes, where are we going?" Janet echoed the question.

"For a drive," Reese responded cryptically.

They drove for about an hour, the scenery breathtaking. Fall aspen colors of brilliant yellow set against tall dark pine trees and snowcapped mountains had to be one of the most beautiful sights on God's earth.

"I love this drive," Janet murmured after a while, in awe of such beauty. Reese took her hand and squeezed it, his eyes smiling deeply into hers.

An hour later he turned off the main road down a dirt one that led far into the trees. After what seemed an eternity they stopped in front of a log cabin nestled on the side of a mountain.

"Yours?" Janet asked with a sense of astonishment. Here was another side of Reese she didn't know. Before, she had seen him as a man who ate chateaubriand, who enjoyed the opera and . . . she paused and smiled, French movies.

"Mine," he assured her. "And you assumed all those Monday mornings I came in late that I was returning from wild weekend parties."

She had thought that, several times. "I did, how'd you know?"

Reese laughed, helping her out of the car and linking his hand with hers. "Because your mouth would thin and your eyes would spark with indignation and righteousness."

"I would not!" she denied forcefully.

He kissed the tip of her nose. "I thought you Christians weren't supposed to lie?"

"I don't lie," Joel stated proudly, wanting to be included in the conversation. "But Jimmy Jones does. I found him out. I prayed and asked Jesus to forgive him."

"That was very thoughtful of you, Joel."

"It was you who told me to." Joel was looking at her funny. "Are you all right, Janny?"

"I'm fine." She looked at Reese, all her love shining in her face. "I'm very fine."

It was a day Janet would remember and cherish all her life. Nothing could have made it more perfect. They hiked, they joked, they laughed and sang songs. Janet and Joel taught Reese some of the songs from the church youth group and watched as Reese burst into laughter.

"Give me salt for my Fritos because the Lord is neato, neato?" Reese repeated with disbelief.

Joel laughed, the sound high-pitched and enthusiastic. "Give me gas for my Ford, I want to keep trucking for the Lord." He led the next verse.

Reese hadn't kissed or held Janet all day, and yet she was vibrantly aware of him. Charged currents of electricity arced between them with a gentle look that became a caress, then a soft brushing of their hands. They didn't need words or kisses or anything else.

Exhausted, Joel fell asleep in the backseat during the drive home.

"Happy?" Reese asked her. One hand was on the steering wheel while the other held her close to his side.

Janet's head rested against the crook of his arm. "Oh yes," she murmured.

"It looks like Joel's asleep."

A lazy, contented smile flickered across her face. "He hasn't been this quiet since the day he was born, except when he's asleep."

Chuckling, Reese tightened his hold. "I like your brother. You're quite a bit alike."

Janet tensed and released a long sigh. "Just a few years ago I would have been offended by that. Now I consider it a compliment."

"What was different in the past?"

Janet snuggled more securely in his embrace. "I was different. I was almost ten when Joel was born. I can remember how desperately my parents wanted another child and my mother's repeated miscarriages. We were all so excited and happy when she became pregnant with Joel. Then when he was born we knew right away he was different. The only time I've ever seen my father cry was the day my brother was born. It seemed so unfair."

"I can understand how you felt."

Janet didn't doubt the sincerity of his comment. "In the beginning I was ashamed of Joel. I didn't want him, didn't want to be associated with him. If it had been up to me I would have put him in an institution and forgotten about him. Thank the Lord, my mom and dad saw things differently."

"But you're proud of him now, aren't you?"

"Fiercely proud. Joel has overcome obstacles that boggle the mind. His biggest obstacle being his sister."

Janet could sense more than see Reese's surprise. "In the beginning I didn't want to have anything to do with him. I wouldn't hold or touch him. Later, against everything I wanted to feel, I found myself loving this defenseless child. But I was full of anger. Anger at my parents for whatever reason; I'm not sure. At first I blamed them for Joel's condition. Mom was older. She should have recognized the risks of having a Down's syndrome baby. But, more directly, I was angry with God. He was the one who had done this to my brother. Maybe I wouldn't have felt so strongly if my parents could have had a house full of children. But they weren't greedy; they only wanted one other child. I couldn't understand it, especially when Dad and Mom had served the Lord all their lives. Was this their reward for being faithful?" She stopped and straightened. "I'm sorry, I didn't mean to talk up a storm. You must find all this boring."

"Not at all," he contradicted her. "What happened to change your mind?"

"Joel," she laughed softly. "He grew up, struggling with things that you and I take for granted. Tying his shoes, counting and learning his ABCs. But he's mastered every skill and praised God for every accomplishment. One day when I was about eighteen he came to me and said something profound. Joel looked at me and said, 'Janny, God doesn't have any grandchildren.'"

"What did he say?" Reese questioned, and Janet repeated the statement.

"I don't know where he came up with that. But what he said was true. For the first time in my life I owned up to the fact I wasn't going to gain eternal life on my parents' coattails. I'd been fighting God for so long, fighting my parents. It's amazing to me now to think that one statement from my brother could change so much in my life. But I was ready to make my peace with God and accept His plan for Joel's life and my own. I was ready to trust."

"Was your rebellion all due to your brother?"

"Heavens no. Oh, a large part of it was, but the pressure put upon me to be the model Christian because my father is a minister was unbelievable. I hated it and did my best to be just the opposite."

Reese was quiet for the remainder of the trip home. He dropped off Joel first and declined her parents' invitation to come inside. Neither did he stay when Janet issued the same invitation later at her apartment. His kiss outside her door was gentle and so tender that Janet savored it for hours afterward.

On Monday morning Janet dressed with extra care and kept her hair down. It was something she rarely did, but she knew Reese preferred it down and she wanted to please him.

The minute she walked into the office she

sensed that something wasn't right. "Is that you, Miss Montgomery?" Reese barked.

"Yes . . . yes, it is." She finished hanging up her coat and walked into his office.

"Order flowers for Bunny Jacobs," he commanded, his eyes not meeting hers. "Something special."

"Right away," she responded crisply. Something was wrong, something was very wrong.

Chapter Six

Twitching the end of her nose in an effort to restrain her glasses, Janet paused, removed her hands from the keyboard and pushed the irritating frames upward. She examined the letter she was typing, pausing to look at the computer monitor for mistakes. There were more of those than ever lately. The date at the top of the letter seemed to flash on and off like a neon sign. November, a week from Thanksgiving. It was unbelievable. It had only been a month since that day at Reese's cabin. Yet it felt like ten long grueling years.

The Monday following their outing, Janet had immediately sensed that something was dreadfully wrong. Reese was short-tempered and formal with a stilted politeness as he issued orders all morning. Three times he gave her instructions to reach Bunny, talking to the blonde for long periods during the day.

Janet didn't know what had happened to cause this abrupt change in Reese, but by Tuesday she knew she had to find out. Returning from lunch, she walked into his office and closed the door.

Reese looked up, his mouth pinched with irritation. "I didn't ask for you, Miss Montgomery." He hadn't called her Janet since bringing her back to her apartment and kissing her that Saturday night.

"Perhaps not, but I want to know what's going on." She silently congratulated herself on how even and unemotional her voice sounded.

"What's going on?" His thick brows quirked upward, his look arrogant, almost jeering. "I'm trying to run a business."

"I meant, what's going on with us?" Although she remained standing, her hands were tightly clenched in front of her as if to brace herself for what was coming.

"Us?" One dark brow arched higher. "Is there an us?"

He spoke with such sarcasm that a freezing cold began to seep through her heart, paralyzing her for an instant. "I thought—"

"You thought?" His eyes filled with disdain as he stood, leaning forward with the palms of his hands resting on the edge of the desk. "I'd be interested in knowing exactly what you thought. Surely you didn't believe this weekend meant anything?"

121

A numbness spread over her. Without blinking she held his harsh gaze. "I'm afraid I did."

He crossed his arms in front of him. "Then I owe you an apology."

"An apology?" she repeated, the words somehow making it past the block of pain that filled her throat.

Reese stared at his hands as if unable to meet her eyes. "I didn't mean for you to take any of this seriously."

Janet took a deep breath and stiffened. "Then rest assured it will never happen again." She turned away, the terrible coldness in her heart filling her whole being.

"Janet." He stopped her, but she refused to turn around, refused to give him the satisfaction of seeing the hurt in her eyes. "A man becomes accustomed to a certain kind of woman." His voice softened somewhat. "It's sometimes better that way."

Better for who? her mind screamed. Certainly not her.

Ben was picking up Gail after work to go shopping for engagement rings, so Janet walked into an empty apartment. Miraculously, she had made it through the afternoon. She felt as though she were in a state of shock, outside herself, like a stranger watching what was going on around her. There was no physical pain, but the agony ran so deep it seemed to reach into her soul and wrap its way around her.

Opening her purse, she took out the letter of resignation she had typed after talking to Reese. Her intention had been to place it on his desk after he left the office so that he would find it first thing in the morning. Twice she'd placed it there and just as many times taken it away. The last time she had gotten to the parking lot and turned around and gone back for it.

She stared at herself in the mirror, accusing the pale reflection of being weak, spineless. Her head throbbed with such an intense pain she could feel every heartbeat, every breath.

Opening the bathroom cabinet, she took down the aspirin, opened the cap and shook two tablets into the palm of her hand. For a moment she stared at the aspirin and wondered if she really wanted relief. The pain served a valuable purpose; if it dulled her senses enough she wouldn't think about Reese.

Her head supported by the sofa arm, Janet stretched out and placed her arm protectively across her eyes. What was wrong with her? Why hadn't she handed in her resignation? Was she a masochist? Her motives, even in her own mind, were unclear. As soon as a replacement could be found she should leave Dyna-Flow and never see Reese Edwards again. The thought was unbearable. She had to see him, be around him, even if it meant pain and rejection. She was in love with him. Her head pounded violently, as if reacting to the realization. She was in love with a man who would never love her.

So she stayed with Dyna-Flow and Reese Edwards because she couldn't bear to leave.

The computer monitor stared back at her and Janet glanced away, replacing her fingers on the keyboard to finish the letter. A half hour later she took in the correspondence for Reese's signature. He didn't acknowledge her presence as she set the letters on his desk. Their working relationship was almost the way it had been for two years. Almost. Outwardly their reactions to one another were formal, crisp, businesslike. But the changes in Janet weren't ones that could be seen. She thanked God for that. She thanked God for a lot of things these days. Incredible as it may seem, she was grateful to Reese, as he had awakened her to womanhood. It would have been so easy to allow bitterness and resentment to taint her outlook. And she continued to pray for Reese, although she was certain he wouldn't want her prayers had he known.

"Hello, Miss Montgomery." Bunny Jacobs strolled into the office. Janet had seen a lot more of Bunny these last weeks, more than she had any other of Reese's blondes.

"Good afternoon. Reese is in his office; you may go in."

Janet smiled to herself as Bunny walked into the

124

room. The blonde wore the tightest-fitting blue jeans imaginable, with a loud purple sweater and matching three-inch heels. Although she presented a facade of sweet naiveté, Janet had long since recognized Bunny as shrewd and cunning. This girl was after Reese and determined to have him. The thought had the ability to terrify Janet, but she knew Reese, and she had seen him outmanipulate ten blondes with the same idea. He wasn't easily duped and she didn't doubt that he'd seen past the slick facade. However, Bunny had lasted longer than most.

"I'll be out of the office the rest of the afternoon," Reese informed her, moving into her portion of the office. Bunny's arm was looped through his, her eyes smiling up at him adoringly.

"I'll finish this statement and have it on your desk before I leave," Janet replied in an efficient tone, purposely avoiding looking at the two of them linked together. "Is there anything else?"

"No, that'll be fine. Have a nice weekend."

"Thank you, I will."

Monday morning the entire company was buzzing with the plans for the annual Dyna-Flow Ski Adventure, a tradition the elder Mr. Edwards had begun the first years after establishing the business. Colorado was blessed with some of the best skiing in the world. As a "thank-you" to their employees, Dyna-Flow arranged a weekend at

Steamboat Springs every winter. Gail and Janet were novice skiers, but the resort offered a kaleidoscope of winter activities and the two spent only a small portion of the weekend on the slopes.

"Are we going?" Gail asked over lunch. A beautiful solitaire diamond sparkled from the ring finger of her left hand.

"That's up to you," Janet claimed before taking a bite from her chicken salad sandwich. "I'm not the one making plans for a wedding."

"Yes, but that's months away. I want to be the traditional June bride."

"Won't Ben mind if you go gallivanting off for the weekend?" Janet was having trouble showing much enthusiasm. She wasn't even certain she wanted to attend this year. She'd go, but only if Gail felt that she really wanted to.

"Ben knows how much I enjoy this time every year. I feel like it's a special time for you and me, and our friendship. We've really had some good times in the past, and I feel like I haven't been as good a friend as you've needed these past months."

A flush of color invaded Janet's cheeks. Gail had been wonderful, there wasn't any other way to describe the support and love given her by her friend. Not once had Gail murmured an "I told you so." Nor had she offered meaningless platitudes. For the most part she had let Janet work out her own feelings and had been available to lend support when needed. Janet realized how difficult it was for Gail to relate to the hurt Janet was experiencing because she was so happy and so much in love with Ben.

"You've been great," Janet told her sincerely. "And if you want to risk life and limb in a hot tub, I'm willing. It's the ski slopes I'm worried about."

The Dyna-Flow Ski Adventure was set for the first weekend in January and mentally Janet marked the date in her mind. She needed to let loose, be free, have a good time. It gave her something to set her sights upon.

Christmas fell on a Friday and Reese had Janet type a memo stating that working the day of Christmas Eve was optional. He did ask her, however, if she could come in for half a day. Janet didn't mind, although the offices were nearly deserted. She would be spending the holidays with her family and they weren't scheduling anything until that evening.

There were several pieces of mail to deal with and letters to type, but nothing vital. Janet finished about eleven, bringing Reese the finished documents for his signature.

He was sitting in the high-backed leather chair, hands behind his head, watching Janet as she approached. In the past, Janet had noticed, he had avoided direct eye contact with her, but not today. His gaze slowly appraised her, studying her face, the way her dress fit over the slender womanly curves and stopped above her knees, revealing shapely legs. Unable to meet his eyes, afraid of what her expression would reveal, Janet lowered her gaze.

"Is there anything else?" she questioned, her voice slightly breathless.

"Yes, this." Reese pulled open a desk drawer and took out a small, beautifully wrapped box. "Merry Christmas, Janet."

Midnight blue eyes widened with shock. Reese had never given her a personal gift at Christmas. Like every other employee, she received the usual Christmas bonus.

He held it out to her. "Go ahead, open it."

With fingers that shook, Janet untied the bow and removed the multicolored foil paper. She paused as she noted the name of an expensive jeweler etched in gold across a black velvet case. Now it wasn't only her fingers but her whole body that trembled as she opened the lid. A beautiful gold necklace lay in a bed of plush velvet. She raised it, and as she did the square piece of gold that dangled from the end of the chain fell into her hand. She examined it with a puzzled frown. Its design was unusual.

"It's supposed to be a microchip," Reese explained, removing the delicate chain from her trembling fingers. "I wanted to show my appreciation for all the troubles the computer has given you. I know it wasn't easy for you to make the switch."

"But you didn't need . . . I mean, this is much too expensive." Janet didn't need an expert eye to recognize that the microchip was made of solid gold. She was flustered, uneasy.

"I'll be the judge of that."

Janet forced herself to smile. "It's beautiful. I'll treasure it always." She felt so close to tears, the control on her emotions a fragile thread.

"Turn around, I'll put it on for you."

Janet did as he asked, closing her eyes and pressing her lips together as he gently laid the necklace against her throat. Bending her head slightly forward, she hoped to aid him as he hooked the finely spun gold chain. His contact with her skin was brief, yet even the fleeting touch of fingers against her neck left a heated sensation. He was so close that Janet could breath in the tangy pine scent of his after-shave. So close, she reminded herself mentally, and yet so far away.

"I'm finished." His words broke the spell.

Slowly Janet opened her eyes and turned around, her fingers investigating the gift. "Thank you, Reese—" She caught herself in time, and cast her gaze downward. "Mr. Edwards."

"Merry Christmas, Janet." His voice was so soft it was a caress, as gentle and sweet as if he had taken her in his arms and held her close.

"Merry Christmas." She had to leave before she

embarrassed them both. Her hand remained at her throat as she took a step backward in retreat. "May the Lord bless you."

She was already into her room when she heard Reese's husky murmur: "And you."

Christmas was a joyous time with Janet's family. Since her parents had lived in several places and worked with different cultures, the celebration was a mixture of French, Mexican and American traditions. And although she couldn't forget Reese completely, her family's support helped to ease her heavy heart.

Monday morning and it was business as usual. Janet wore Reese's gift and noted how he looked to see if it was there when he came into the outer office later that morning. There seemed to be a small gleam of pleasure when he saw that she had worn it.

"I'm going to the warehouse. You can reach me there if anything comes up."

A steady flow of traffic moved in and out of the office all morning. Malcolm Hayes needed help locating a business report. He had no sooner gone when the senior Mr. Edwards sauntered in.

"Morning, Janet." He beamed her a pleasant smile. "How was your Christmas?"

"Very nice, thank you," she replied politely.

"You're going to Steamboat Springs, aren't you? I'm going to need my best girl."

Janet flushed with pleasure. "Yes, I'll be there."

"Good." The word was clipped as he walked past her into the other room.

Just before noon Bunny Jacobs came into the office, her hands full of large packages. "Oh goodness," she said and heaved several boxes onto the chair. "I just adore shopping the after-Christmas sales." She glanced up and smiled sweetly. "I do hope Reese is in. I was hoping he'd take me to lunch."

"I'm sorry, Miss Jacobs, but Mr. Edwards is out of the office," she replied with professional crispness.

Bunny's sigh was filled with disappointment. "Oh dear, and I did want him to see my new ski outfit." Her laugh was delicate and melodious. "I had to have something new for Steamboat. Reese and I are going to have such a wonderful time."

A huge lump formed in the pit of Janet's stomach. Resentment and envy seemed to be burning a hole in her insides. Bunny was going to Steamboat Springs with Reese. Why should that bother her? Reese had brought a blonde bombshell with him last year, at least that was what she heard. Janet had been so busy with Gail she hadn't seen him the entire weekend. Had she been nurturing some secret hope that he would come alone this year? Unconsciously she straightened, her back stiffening. When was she going to learn? Reese Edwards was never going to

131

be interested in her, and the sooner she accepted the situation the better.

The phone messages were on Janet's desk when Reese returned around noon. He picked them up and sorted through the pink sheets.

"Bunny was in?" he questioned sharply.

Doing her best to appear preoccupied and uncaring, Janet nodded. "Yes, she left these packages and asked if you could bring them by her apartment later."

Reese shrugged. "That's fine. I was planning on seeing her tonight anyway."

After the first day Janet continued to wear Reese's Christmas gift, but she kept it under her sweater, out of sight. It offered a strange comfort, almost symbolic of her love. Like the necklace, her love was disguised, buried beneath a sweater, just as her love was buried deep within her heart.

"Ski Town, U.S.A., here we come," Gail laughed as they boarded one of the buses Dyna-Flow had chartered for the ride to Steamboat Springs. Since many of the employees were bringing their families along, several had opted to drive their own vehicles. Reese and Bunny had left earlier that afternoon. It was unusual for Reese to leave early, especially on a Friday, and Janet did her best to battle the waves of jealousy that threatened to overcome her. The Christmas gift had hurt her more than it had helped. It had given her hope when there was none.

Lenny Forrestal from the accounting department boarded the bus with his guitar draped over his shoulder. Tradition demanded that Lenny lead the lively group in songs for the journey north.

"You girls as anxious to take in some of that gorgeous night skiing as me?" he asked as he walked past.

"Not us," Gail and Janet chimed, then laughed uproariously at Lenny's shocked look. Nothing was that funny, but they were both excited and giddy.

Located in Routt National Forest, Steamboat Springs offered some of the best skiing in the world. Over the years the resort had hosted a score of Olympic hopefuls. Janet had heard the snow called champagne powder. A skier's heaven, the twenty-three hundred acres of Rocky Mountain majesty were divided into seventy-three separate trails serviced by thirteen chair lifts. It wasn't only the skiing that made this annual trip so enjoyable. It was laughing with friends, sleigh rides at midnight, staying up all night beside a cozy fire and talking dreams with Gail. It was about this time last year that Gail had first met Ben. Somehow it seemed longer.

After unloading their suitcases in the room, Janet and Gail ventured into the streets, hoping to do some early shopping and make arrangements for the ski rental the next morning.

"These mountains are unbelievable!" Janet said as she breathed in the clean, crisp air. Mt. Werner was in the distance with Storm King Peak and Sunshine Peak lit up for night skiing. "They seem to reach out to me in some mysterious way."

"I know," Gail agreed, "I feel the same thing. It's marvelous." Several shops were open and both girls picked up something small as a remembrance. Walking back to the lodge, Gail mentioned Janet's outfit. "I can't get over how different you look in that coat and hat."

Janet had splurged on a red and white ski outfit. If Bunny could buy a whole wardrobe for one weekend, then she should be able to manage one outfit. The jacket was a brilliant red color with a bold white stripe that ran across the back of the shoulders and down the sleeves. Steamboat Springs had the reputation of being a friendly Western town, and as a surprise, Joel and her parents had presented Janet with a black, wide-rimmed cowboy hat. The contrast between the prim secretary and the attractive fun-loving woman was striking. Several people from the company walked right past Janet without recognizing her.

The next morning Gail and Janet skied Giggle Gulch, one of the easiest slopes available. The snow was fresh and ideal for the sport. Janet managed to make it down several times without a spill, while Gail took one tumble after another.

"Does Ben know he's marrying such a klutz?" Janet teased, helping to slap the accumulated snow off her friend's back.

"Oh yes, Ben knows," came Gail's laughing response. "Come on. I think it's time for me to retire. I don't know about you, but I'm exhausted."

Janet resecured the cowboy hat. "Yes, ma'am," she said in a thick Western drawl.

Halfway back to the Village Inn Gail paused and murmured, "Don't look now, but guess who I see."

For an instant Janet shut her eyes. There was no need for conjecture. It had to be Bunny and Reese. Curiosity wouldn't allow her to not glance up and pretend she hadn't seen them. They were both coming down the slope, Bunny dressed in a hot pink outfit that was almost fluorescent. She was laughing, weaving her way between less experienced skiers. Hcr long blonde hair flew out behind her. Reese followed, swiftly traversing the snow-covered terrain with commanding skill. One glance at the happy couple was like a knife twisting in Janet's heart.

"If it hurts, don't watch," Gail said, laying her hand gently on Janet's shoulder.

It was crazy to torture herself, but she couldn't force herself to look away. "No, I want to see what kind of skier Bunny is."

With Gail at her side, Janet stood apart from the

crowd and waited until Reese and Bunny had gotten back on the chair lift. It was easy to follow their progress with Bunny's bright pink outfit lighting the way. Finally, they were out of sight. She didn't know how long it would take before they came down the slope, but Janet was prepared to wait.

A long time later Janet recognized the couple weaving their way down the slope. She swallowed tightly. Bunny was fantastic, absolutely fearless as she agilely manipulated her body over the moguls, snow spitting out from beside her.

"Come on." Gail tugged at her arm. "You've seen enough. Besides, I'm getting cold."

Tossing one last envious glance over her shoulder, Janet continued toward the Village Inn. Wasn't it enough that Bunny had Reese? It was unfair that she was a gifted skier besides. Janet paused and looked to the bright, blue skies, almost angry with God. There didn't seem to be any justice left in the world.

A half hour later, sitting around a large table drinking hot cocoa with several others from Dyna-Flow, the pain of seeing Reese and Bunny began to ease.

Dressed in a ski cap and gray cable-knit sweater, Samuel Edwards joined the group. "There's my best girl." He sat beside Janet, who scooted to make room for the older man in the upholstered booth. "You're looking mighty pretty these days," he chided, squeezing her hand. There seemed to be a murmur of agreement from the others sharing the booth.

"Thank you, Mr. Edwards."

"None of that formal stuff here. We'll save that for the office. You call me Sam, like everyone else."

A smile hovered over her lips. Calling the elder Mr. Edwards by his first name was as unnatural as referring to the U.S. president as Ronnie, instead of President Reagan. "If you insist."

"I do, my dear."

Gradually the group dwindled down until there was only Gail, Janet and Sam Edwards. "It looks like everyone is having a good time."

"We are, it's marvelous," Janet confirmed.

"Excuse me a minute. I'll be right back." Gail slid out of the seat and headed toward the ladies' room.

Janet's gaze followed her friend; she felt slightly uneasy sitting alone with Reese's father. Her gaze centered on the mug of chocolate she was cupping with her hands. At the sound of an angry snort Janet looked up. Reese and Bunny had come inside. Apparently they chose to ignore Janet and Reese's father and chose a booth on the other side of the room.

"What's wrong with that son of mine?" Samuel Edwards murmured, his head tilting in the direction of his son across the room. "What is it he sees in these blondes? Dating one after the other. I should be a grandfather several times over by now and all Reese cares about is . . ." He let the rest of what he was going to say fade away.

Bunny and Reese were sitting beside one another. Reese's arm was casually draped over Bunny's shoulders while they stared lovingly into one another's eyes.

Janet unconsciously bit into her bottom lip to prevent a rush of pain from slipping out. When Reese lowered his head and gently placed his lips over Bunny's, Janet thought she would die. Unable to watch, she jerked her face around and closed her eyes until the searing pain passed. When she looked up again, Samuel Edwards was studying her closely. She couldn't bear it, not for another moment.

"Please . . ." She slid from the booth. "I must leave." Her knees were shaking as she hurried out the door.

"Where are you going?" Gail ran after her.

Janet looked around her wildly. "Skiing. We're here to ski, aren't we?"

"Yes . . . but—"

"That's the problem with my whole life." Tears welled in the depth of her eyes, threatening to spill. "I live in a nice, packaged little box, I never let loose."

"Janet"—Gail said her name thoughtfully— "what happened? Why are you crying?"

"I'm not," she protested. "It's the cold. My eyes always water when it's this chilly."

"What are you doing?" Gail demanded when Janet snapped her boots into the skies. "You've already been skiing; you're exhausted."

"I'm not, I'm invigorated. I'm going to allow a little adventure into my life. I'm . . . I'm going to ski Priest Creek."

"Priest Creek?" Gail repeated with an astonished gasp. "You're crazy! That's an advanced course, one of the most difficult. You'll be killed up there."

"Listen, friend, I'm a lot better skier than you realize," Janet insisted. "I was sticking around the easier slopes so you wouldn't be alone. I'm headed for the big time now."

"Janet, you can't." There was a frantic edge to Gail's voice.

"Just watch me," Janet shouted and without a backward glance she headed for the Priest Creek chair lift.

The double chair extended almost two thousand feet vertically. Janet sat, her hand desperately clenching the metal frame. A tear spilled down her face and she furiously wiped it aside. She may not be another Jean-Claude Killy, but it wasn't from lack of trying.

As the chair progressed up the mountain, Janet watched the skiers slice their way through the snow far below. This was the intermediate course and already she could see it was far beyond her skill. She held her breath. If this was the intermediate slope, what would the advanced be like? More unsettling was the thought that there was only one way down.

It wasn't crowded at the top, not like it had been in the other areas. Janet paused, looking down the slope. It was steep, steeper than she had ever imagined. This wasn't the type of course where she could progress slowly downward. She would need to twist and curve her way. She stopped and looked over the slope again. It was a long way to the bottom, a very long way. The wind whipped up tiny particles of snow and as Janet stared into the clear blue sky they looked like small bits of floating blue crystal.

It had been pure lunacy to attempt this run, Janet realized, but it was too late. Far too late. Her heart was hammering wildly and her palms were sweating. For a second she paused to murmur a desperate prayer.

Heaving a giant breath, Janet's gloved hands dug her poles into the snow as she lunged forward. She knew it would be important to keep up her speed. Mentally she reviewed everything she had learned over the past years, refusing to dwell on the seriousness of her predicament.

Thirty feet from the top and she took her first tumble. Stunned, she lay twisted in the snow, uncertain what had happened. She sat helplessly for a few minutes, shaking with fright as skilled skiers whipped past, throwing pitying glances over their shoulders.

"You can do it," she told herself, audibly mumbling the words. "Don't look down . . . don't look down."

Her knees were shaking once she was upright again. She forced herself to start, using her ski poles to push off. If she hadn't been so frightened the course would have been exhilarating, her senses vibrantly alive. But the only thing Janet sensed now was the danger she had gotten herself into.

The second fall came only minutes later. She wrenched her ankle and bit into the fleshy part of her bottom lip to keep from crying. Experience told her she wasn't badly hurt. Slowly she righted herself and gently tested her ankle. The course ahead was full of heavy moguls and complicated twists and curves that were far beyond her experience or capabilities.

The thought came that she could die right here and no one would know or care. Several others whizzed past with no inkling of her situation.

"Show a little mettle," she chastised herself out loud. "You are going to ski off this mountain and arrive in one piece and prove to the whole world how wonderful you really are." The thought was so ludicrous she almost laughed. There wasn't a thing she wanted to prove to anyone. If anyone needed proof, it was herself and the test was now!

Every move was deliberate and exaggerated as Janet skied as far to the right as possible in order to stay away from the other skiers. She didn't want to distract or trip them with her bumbling movements. She had long since lost her precious cowboy hat. It lay in the snow twenty feet above her, but it might as well have been twenty miles.

Her mouth felt dry. The dehydrated feeling extended all the way down her throat, so that every swallow became painful, as if something was grating against her larynx.

A hundred feet from the top and she took her third tumble. Her left ski shot out from under her and she fell sideways, her shoulder receiving the brunt of the fall. The right ski was at an awkward angle behind her and she spent several tedious minutes straightening her leg and ski.

The feeling of panic was so strong that she began to shake with it. Barely a hundred feet from the top and she had already fallen three times; the run was almost two thousand feet long. How would she ever reach the bottom in one piece? Tears burned in her eyes, only adding to her frustration.

"Oh, Jesus, please," she prayed, "just get me out of this alive." Leaning heavily on her poles she managed to stand up. "You can do it," she told herself, but the words sounded weak and unconvincing. "You can do it," she repeated as if desperately hoping to persuade herself.

She only managed to go a few feet, slowly gathering speed, when she felt her balance give way and she fell backward. Flat on her back in the powdery snow, Janet recalled lying like this as a little girl and moving her arms back and forth to form "angel's wings." She needed an angel right now, a guardian angel. It would be safer for her to take off the skies and crawl off the mountain.

What did people do if they realized they couldn't make it down? Wasn't the ski patrol supposed to be around to help someone like her before she became a mountain casualty? Only yesterday she'd seen them hauling a woman down from the mountain in a wire litter.

What did she have to do to get help? Pulling herself into a sitting position, she looked around her frantically. A few uncaring souls slid past her, but there wasn't anyone with the familiar ski patrol patch that she could see.

Every muscle hurt; she was cold and miserable. "I'm not going to make it," she cried, her voice so weak it was barely audible. "I'm trapped like an animal." She hiccupped on a huge sob and dug one ski pole in the snow to help raise herself. "Keep going, keep going," she mumbled urgently. Gathering her resolve, Janet stood, frustration hunching her shoulders while her poles were poised at her side. She felt a spray of snow splash against her as another skier came to an abrupt halt directly behind her.

"You crazy idiot, what are you doing here?" The contempt in the familiar voice caused Janet to gasp. Her eyes grew round with pain and confusion.

"Reese, oh, Reese," she whispered and burst into tears.

Chapter Seven

"Well?" Reese continued, unaffected by her tears. "Answer me. What are you doing on Priest Creek?" A hard mask stole over his face, tightening the handsome features.

Janet raised a gloved hand to her face and wiped the moisture from her cheek. "I'm skiing," she muttered and released her breath with quivering slowness.

"Skiing?" Reese responded with an underlying tone of cynicism. "From what I've witnessed I can assure you that you are not skiing."

"All right," Janet snapped. "So I'm not an Olympic hopeful."

"An Olympic hopeful?" he breathed in deeply as if to gain control of his anger. "I have seen cartoons of Donald Duck skiing with more finesse than you."

"Wonderful," she said and sniffled. "Go watch cartoons. I don't need you; someone from the ski patrol will be along any minute."

Standing like a warlord above her, Reese grew dark and forbidding.

"Go on," she prompted. "Leave me alone." Her chin tilted at a proud angle, Janet felt safe. Reese wouldn't really abandon her. Not when he recognized what precarious straits she'd gotten herself into.

Reese made a movement as if to leave and Janet watched, stunned. Only moments before she had been desperately praying for help. Now she was sending the only available rescuer away. It was pride that had gotten her into this mess. A verse from Proverbs shot through her mind: "Pride goeth before destruction, and a haughty spirit before a fall." In this case the words could be translated literally.

A group of skiers whipped past them, kicking up the champagne-quality snow. Janet turned her face aside. Before she had the chance to say another word, Reese dug his ski poles into the snow and went around her. "Sorry, I was mistaken. I thought you were in trouble."

Frantically she called after him. "Reese, please . . ." Moisture filled her eyes as she helplessly watched him ski around the curve and disappear. "Oh no, now you've really done it, Janet Lynn Montgomery." She slammed one of her ski poles into the snow and inhaled a shaky breath.

Carefully she began again, making her descent

as slow as possible, yet realizing it would be necessary to build up her speed to make it over the moguls. Another skier flew past her.

"Help," she called out as loud as she could. "Please, won't someone help me?" Each word dwindled in volume until the last word was almost a whisper.

She took another tumble as soon as she made it around the first curve. Stunned, she lay in the snow, catching her breath. With deliberate care she tested her arms and legs to be sure she was all right.

Sitting up, Janet looked around her for help. What did people call when they needed assistance.

"Help!" She screamed at the top of her lungs. Her call was immediately lost in a huge vacuum of quiet. "Help," she repeated, cupping her hands alongside of her mouth, hoping to increase the range of her urgent voice.

She waited. Nothing.

Groaning, Janet lay back in the snow and in childlike fashion moved her arms back and forth to form angel's wings.

Another skier approached. "Help," she called again, sitting up and waving her arms above her head.

Nothing. Whoever it was didn't so much as glance her way. Uncaring nerd! Janet thought unkindly. Analyzing her situation, she realized that if anything, she was worse off than before.

Obviously no one cared. Screaming for help was getting her nowhere.

Janet could see someone else approaching in the distance. Desperate straits demand desperate measures. Waving her hands, she screamed as loudly as possible, "Medic!"

A familiar deep-throated chuckle sounded below her. The terrain was so steep that Reese had been only a few feet down the slope from her and she hadn't been able to see him.

"Reese," she cried out, relief filling her voice. With a supreme effort she managed to clumsily stand up again. "Oh, Reese, is that you? I'm sorry, don't go . . . please don't leave me."

Sidestepping up the run toward her, Reese quickly came into view. "Are you willing to admit you need me?" The anger was gone from his eyes, replaced with a teasing glitter.

"Yes, oh yes."

He stood almost directly in front of her. "This is a fine mess you've gotten yourself into, Janet Montgomery."

Her long, dark lashes fluttered downward. Her pride was gone, crumbled and shattered with the last spill. At this point, Janet decided, she didn't care what she had to admit as long as she got off the mountain alive. "I do ski like Donald Duck."

Only a second passed before the tantalizing brush of his mouth over hers caught her unaware and Janet lost her balance. Her hands flew out to her side as she started to fall backward. In a futile effort to steady her, Reese reached out to prevent the inevitable and was propelled into the snow with her. Dazed, they stared into one another's eyes for a long moment.

"You okay?" Reese questioned, positioned above her, his hands braced on either side of her face.

"Sure." Her mouth curved into a rueful smile. "What's one more tumble when I've experienced so many?"

Reese smiled, but seemed reluctant to move. His gaze roamed over her face, and for an instant all time came to a screeching halt. Slowly he lowered his head, kissing first the corner of her eye, then her cheek, and her nose, finally reaching her soft, parted mouth.

Janet moaned, accepting his kiss. Nothing had ever been so sweet, so beautiful. So wonderful.

Gradually Reese raised his head, his eyes filled with the same wonder Janet was sure was a reflection of her own. Removing his glove, Reese lightly caressed her cheek. His touch spread an encompassing warmth that reached deep within her heart.

When his mouth closed fiercely over hers, Janet couldn't contain the small welcoming sigh. Her blood pounded in her veins, keeping pace with the frenzied beat of her heart.

"No . . . no," she whispered urgently and jerked

her face away from him How could she forget so easily? How could she allow him to do this to her again? Only a few minutes before he had been kissing Bunny with the same abandon. Janet didn't need to be told she was only a convenient distraction.

His breathing irregular and slightly ragged, Reese raised his head and removed his imprisoning hands. His lean fingers were buried into the shoulders of her thick red jacket as he aided Janet into a sitting position beside him. They didn't speak for several long, grating moments.

"Are you ready?" Reese asked as he stood.

Janet looked away, afraid her feelings would radiate from her face. "As ready as I'll ever be." Her voice was hoarse and aching.

He talked to her for several minutes, giving her instructions. He would go first and she must follow, doing exactly as he did. Working together, they would arrive safely at the bottom of the run. Janet wished she felt as confident as Reese sounded.

He took off ahead of her and Janet did her best to imitate his moves. It wasn't easy, although she went farther than before without falling. Several hundred feet later she missed a turn and plowed into the snow. Quickly she sat up and attempted to balance herself so Reese could see she wasn't hurt.

Gradually, he sidestepped his way back to her side.

"Are you hurt?" he called, the timbre of his voice rocking over her.

"No . . . I'm fine," she muttered and breathed shakily.

Halfway down the run she took another spill, losing one ski and a pole.

Reese retrieved them for her, bringing the equipment back and snapping her boot to the skis. "We're going to make it. You're doing great."

Janet attempted a weak laugh. "You don't tell a woman who's looking death in the eye that she's doing great."

A frown marred his brow. "I mean it."

Janet couldn't doubt the sincerity, although she found it amusing.

"Janet, look at me," he ordered.

She couldn't do as he asked. "I'm frightened," she whispered.

"I know, but I'll get you down if I have to toss you over my shoulder and haul you myself."

"I'm sure I'll reach the bottom. The question is: Will I be dead or alive?" Her laugh was breathless.

"Alive," Reese said with crisp confidence.

It wasn't easy. There was never a moment that Janet felt completely safe until the Village Inn was in view.

Gail was outside pacing back and forth, forming

a path in the snow as she waited for her. A worried frown creased her smooth brow. "You idiot," she muttered angrily the minute she reached Janet. "I've been worried sick."

"I think she's learned her lesson," Reese intervened. "Take her back to your room and see that she takes a hot bath."

Gail's look was narrowed and testy as she turned around to glare at Reese. "As far as I'm concerned this is all your doing."

"Gail." Janet choked with embarrassment and quickly leaned down to remove her skis.

Her friend's fiery gaze shot from one to the other. She looped her arm through Janet's and directed her toward the Village Inn. "You must have been frightened out of your wits."

Janet sighed expressively. "You don't know the half of it."

A half hour later Janet was relaxing in the tub, her head resting against the white porcelain back as the hot water soothed her aching muscles. In a dreamlike state, she remembered the feel of Reese's mouth over hers. Tentatively her wet fingers outlined her lips. It was so difficult to believe that Reese had been anything but candid when he kissed her. The aching look in his eyes had confirmed as much. And yet she knew better. Desperately she wanted to believe Reese really did feel something for her, but to do so was utter foolishness. What Gail had said months before returned to haunt her. Janet was convinced that Reese was sincere and Gail had reminded her that was what each one of his women assumed. Perhaps he was one of those men who could never love only one woman. As soon as the thought was formed, Janet recognized the truth. There would always be women in Reese's life and always more than one.

By dinnertime Janet was famished. She hadn't eaten since breakfast, but she discarded Gail's suggestion that they have something sent to their room and enjoy a quiet dinner. The dining room was sure to be the hub of activity and Janet needed an escape from the introspection that Gail might force upon her.

The lodge dining room was full of employees from Dyna-Flow. Only vaguely aware of what she was doing, Janet searched the crowds, seeking Reese. She swallowed with difficulty when she saw him and Bunny on the far side of the room.

The eating area was an informal one with a huge stone fireplace, polished wooden floors and a small section for dancing in the center.

Gail and Janet were seated at a table for four and were quickly joined by two single men from Dyna-Flow.

"You don't mind, do you?" Lenny Forrestal asked, taking the seat beside Janet. "The place is getting crowded. I can't see taking up two tables when we can share this one."

"No, we don't mind." Gail answered for them both, casting a knowing glance Janet's way. Lenny had the reputation of being a flirt, but a nice flirt.

By the time they finished their meal the music had started and several couples were dancing.

"Shall we?" Lenny looked at Janet.

"All right." She stood and with Lenny's hand guiding her they weaved through the tables to the tiny dance floor. The crowded floor left little room to maneuver, and more from necessity than desire Janet was pressed tightly against Lenny's chest.

He was attentive and pleasant and Janet found herself laughing at his wit and humor. He wasn't as compelling or as exciting as Reese but . . . she refused to allow the comparison to continue. She couldn't daydream about Reese when he was in the same room with another woman. Unwillingly her eyes sought them out.

"What do you think of the boss's bombshell?" Lenny questioned unexpectedly, seeming to follow her gaze.

Janet looked away abruptly. "If you've seen one, you've seen them all."

Lenny's laugh was loud enough to embarrass Janet and create unnecessary attention. His hands slid around her waist, fingers linked at the base of her spine, bringing her closer than Janet wished. Using her hands as leverage, she pushed against his chest, creating an inch of space between them.

For the moment Lenny accepted her reluctance. At the end of the dance they were caught in the crowd.

"Would you like to keep on dancing?" he suggested.

"No thanks," Janet said sweetly but firmly.

"You can't blame a guy for trying," Lenny teased.

"This dance is mine." From out of nowhere, Janet was pulled from Lenny's embrace and into Reese's arms. The hold was punishing as a hard circle of arms enveloped her.

The action had been so unexpected that for a moment Janet was speechless. "Why did you do that?" she demanded.

Reese's mouth was twisted in an uncompromising line. "I didn't like the way he was handling you."

Janet's blue eyes rounded indignantly. "You didn't like? Listen, Mr. Edwards," her voice dipped with the formal use of his name, "I'm perfectly capable of handling Lenny Forrestal, or any other man for that matter."

"Just like you're capable of skiing Priest Creek?" His upper lip curved into a snarl, his eyes harsh.

Janet stopped the pretense of dancing and pushed his hands loose. "I don't know what it is about you, Reese," she said in a quiet voice that trembled with emotion. "You can make me angrier than I've ever known I could be. Save your caveman tactics for Bunny. I don't want them."

"Leave Bunny out of this," he ordered in an ominously low voice.

To hear him so readily jump to the blonde's defense created a new ache within her heart. "Gladly." She turned sharply to leave and almost cried with frustration. She was trapped in a heavy throng of early evening partygoers who were moving about on the tiny dance floor. Without looking back, bit by bit she eased herself from the crowd and the table where Gail, Lenny and Thom Aaron were waiting.

Burning color invaded her cheeks as Janet felt Lenny's piercing eyes studying her closely.

"I didn't know you and Edwards had a thing going," he muttered the minute she sat down.

"We don't," she denied.

Lenny's eyes were disbelieving and he rubbed one side of his face with his hand. "It certainly looked that way to me. I had the feeling he would have easily broken my jaw, given the slightest provocation."

"I'm sure you're mistaken," Janet murmured, avoiding his gaze. Reese was harder to understand by the minute. The Saturday morning he had taken her to his cabin he seemed reluctant to have anyone from Dyna-Flow, even Gail, know that he was seeing her. Now he was making an issue of it on a crowded dance floor.

"I'm ready to leave if you are," Gail leaned across the table and whispered.

Janet had never been more grateful to her friend. "Yes, please."

They made their excuses and amid polite protests returned to the lodge.

Monday morning everything had returned to normal. Janet arrived at the office at the usual time, but the door between the two rooms was tightly shut. Reese hadn't made it in yet.

The coffee was brewed and the mail sorted, and still Reese hadn't arrived. Maybe he was ill. Although he'd been late on several Mondays, he'd never arrived this late. By ten a worried Janet decided to call his home, something she rarely did. There was no answer.

Samuel Edwards sauntered into the office around eleven. Janet looked up, relieved. After the weekend she had decided to play the unemotional, indifferent secretary, to greet Reese coolly. But if he'd walked into the office at that moment she would have had to restrain herself from throwing her arms around him.

"What's the matter, Janet?" Samuel Edwards was astute enough to instantly recognize her distress no matter how hard she attempted to disguise it.

"Mr. Edwards hasn't arrived yet." She unconsciously bit into her lip. "There are several meetings scheduled this afternoon and I'm not sure what to do. Should I cancel everything? I . . . I wasn't aware. I mean, he didn't say anything about not coming in today."

Even Samuel Edwards appeared surprised. "That's not like Reese." His look was thoughtful. "Have you tried phoning that blonde's place?"

A freezing cold stole over Janet and she lowered her eyes. "I . . . I'd rather not do that, Mr. Edwards. I believe your son's private life should be private and I don't think it's my position to involve myself." If Reese had spent the night with Bunny, Janet didn't want to know it. "I think you understand."

The elder Edwards nodded, his features giving the impression of gently understanding. "Of course I do."

"Could Reese be at the cabin?"

Samuel Edwards glanced up surprised. "Cabin, what cabin? Reese doesn't have a cabin, at least not one I know about."

The freezing chill Janet had felt before seemed to settle itself around her heart. "I believe he's mentioned a log cabin near Black Hawk."

"I'm sure you must be mistaken. If Reese had some retreat, then I'd know it."

Janet was barely conscious of the remainder of the conversation. That whole beautiful day she had spent with Reese last autumn had been a farce. He had lied to her, led her to believe he sought peace and serenity in a mountain hideaway. Why? Her mind tossed the question around. Janet didn't want to recognize the truth. Reese knew she would love the cabin too. Perhaps he felt she would give herself to him if he . . . she stopped, hating what she was thinking. That couldn't be right. He was the one who had pulled back from making love to her. But why? Reese Edwards was so complicated; Janet realized she would never understand him. For two years she had been witness to the contradictions in him. He could be a cunning business tycoon and unbelievably blind about women. She had seen looks from him that made men shake, and yet he was gentle and patient with Joel. He had held her in his arms, fighting his natural desire for her, then he'd been cold and cruel only hours later. No, she would never understand this man. It was better if she quit trying.

At five Janet cleared off her desk. What would she do tomorrow if Reese didn't show? She'd been able to rearrange his meetings and reschedule appointments, but she couldn't continue to do so without serious repercussions.

Ben came to pick up Gail after dinner. The couple was receiving marriage counseling from Stewart Montgomery.

"Give Dad my love," Janet said as they walked out the door.

"Have you told them you lost the cowboy hat yet?" Gail questioned with a teasing glint to her dark eyes.

Janet flinched. "Not yet. Joel's going to give me a lecture that will last a lifetime. I think I'll wait until I can catch him in a good mood."

"Good idea." The door closed and Janet was left to face another night alone. With Gail so busy with the wedding plans, Janet was alone nights more than ever. Usually she didn't mind, it gave her an opportunity to do things she normally wouldn't do. But lately she spent more time steering her thoughts away from Reese. How easy it would be to let him dominate every waking minute. But she couldn't allow it to happen, it was dangerous, far too dangerous.

The doorbell chimed a half hour later and Janet answered with her purse in her hand. It was probably the paperboy come to collect.

"Reese." Her voice was a strange, strangled sound that was an odd mixture of surprise and bewilderment.

He stood in the open doorway, casually dressed, a wry smile twisting his mouth.

Confused and muddled, Janet didn't know whether to shout at him for worrying her all day with his disappearing act or throw her arms around him because she was so glad he was safe and unhurt.

"Can I come in?"

"Of course." She moved aside. "I'm sorry, it's just that I'm so surprised to see you." Her mind was screaming at him, demanding an explanation. She bit into her lip to keep from hurling accusations. If he had been with Bunny she didn't want to know.

He raked his hands through his hair and took off his jacket, placing it over the back of the sofa.

If Janet didn't know better she'd say that he looked reluctant, uneasy. His mouth was pinched, his eyes dull. She placed a silken strand of hair around her ear. "I suppose you're wondering what I did about the appointments you had for today," she began, her voice slightly shaky.

"No." The word was clipped, almost angry.

Still standing, Janet took a step back, pretending she hadn't heard. "I phoned Bob Pratt at the warehouse and made arrangements to have—"

"Janet," he demanded, his expression brooding. "I want to talk to you."

"I'm sure you do. Sit down"—her hand gestured toward the couch—"there's coffee if you'd like a cup."

"I don't want coffee. I don't want to discuss business. And for heaven's sake"—He rammed his fists into his pockets—"will you stop fidgeting like a rabbit. I'm not going to pounce on you."

Hands clenched behind her, Janet backed into the wall. There was that look about him; she had recognized it almost immediately. She'd seen it

160

that night in the parking lot after the movie, again when he had kissed her on Priest Creek. She couldn't trust Reese when he looked at her like that. Worse, she couldn't trust herself.

"Why are you here?" she questioned, her voice trembling slightly. It was vital that she keep her distance. Her awareness of him was growing every second. His presence filled the room.

"I want to talk about us."

"Us?" She repeated the lone word like a recording, drawing in a deep breath.

His blue gaze seemed to pin her down as the lines around his mouth tightened.

A wave of heat invaded her face. He couldn't do this to her, not again. She couldn't bear it. He'd lied to her about the cabin, ruining one of the most beautiful days of her life. He had gone from her arms to Bunny's without regret. Not once, but time after time. No, she wouldn't share him; she was greedy. It had to be all or nothing.

Swiftly she walked into the kitchen, opened the refrigerator and took out the orange juice.

"What are you doing?" He followed her into the cozy room and regarded her movements with a trace of anger in his eyes.

"I'm thirsty," she stammered, her hands visibly shaking as she took down a glass and poured the juice. Tipping her head back, she swallowed. The chilled liquid felt soothing against her dry throat. When she finished she asked again, "Are you sure you wouldn't like something?" Her breathing was unnatural, almost husky.

Reese was standing in the doorway, blocking the entrance, the dark, intense gaze holding her motionless. "Yes, I want something," he said dryly. "I want you to come into the living room, sit down and listen to me."

"Okay." She attempted to sound nonchalant and natural.

His hand at her shoulder, he guided her into the room, gently pushed her into the overstuffed chair and sat on the ottoman so that he was directly in front of her. Taking both her hands into his, he leaned forward, resting his elbows on his knees. His gaze centered on her fingers.

"As I mentioned, I want to talk about us."

A lump formed in her throat and Janet looked away. "I didn't know there was an us." Wasn't that what he had said to her? If she expected any sense of triumph in hurling his own words back at him, she was disappointed. Only an empty, depleted feeling returned.

Reese looked up, shock filling his eyes before he could disguise it.

The phone rang and Janet leaped up to answer it, grateful for an excuse to move away from him. Her back facing Reese, she picked up the receiver.

"Hello."

An embarrassed silence followed. "Sorry, wrong number." The line was disconnected.

"Hello, Gary," she spoke into the receiver. Lying, pretending, she detested it all. Hadn't she done it often enough in the past for Reese? Again there was no sense of exultation in tricking him. "Yes, I'm free Friday." She hesitated, giving the impression that she was listening. The dial tone droned in her ear. "I'd like that. I'd like that very much. I'll look forward to seeing you." Again she paused. "Good-bye." Her hand was shaking as she replaced the receiver. Thankfully, Reese couldn't see how unsettled she was.

Janet heard him stand, could feel the barely restrained anger of his movements behind her.

"Perhaps it would be better if we discussed this another time." His control was unnerving.

"Yes, I think it would." Her sigh was bitter.

"Good night then."

Still she remained poised by the phone, her hand clenching the receiver. Slowly, painfully she lowered her thick lashes.

"Good night, Mr. Edwards."

"Miss Montgomery," he hissed in a voice filled with contempt.

She heard the door slam and her heart shattered like a fragile piece of crystal that had been hurled against a cement wall.

After tonight Reese would hate her; she had willfully injured his pride. His ego wouldn't tolerate such rejection.

For a long time afterward Janet sat on the couch

staring into space. First she tried to force herself to pray and read her Bible, anything to keep her mind off what she had done. Nothing worked. For a time she felt only a numbness. Gradually feeling returned as a haze of pain swirled its way around her. The ache took the form of nagging guilt. Lying to Reese was wrong. Very wrong.

The next morning Janet woke with a throbbing headache. Her fingertips pressed against her temples, she walked into the kitchen.

"Who drank all the orange juice?" Gail questioned, rummaging through the refrigerator.

"Guess?" Janet murmured sarcastically.

It was so unusual for Janet to be out of sorts that Gail paused and turned around. "Are you feeling all right?"

"Wonderful," Janet said, expelling a long sigh. "But I think I have Excedrin headache number two hundred."

"That bad?" Gail questioned, a frown creasing her brow. "Are you sure you feel up to working? I can phone in for you if you like."

"No." Janet dismissed her friend's concern with a short shake of her head, then groaned as fresh pain shot through the top of her skull.

There had never been a time in her life that Janet dreaded seeing anyone more than she did Reese Edwards that morning. Hoping to delay the inevitable as long as possible, she quietly opened the door to her office and tiptoed inside.

Noiselessly she removed her coat and hung it on the hanger before moving across the room to put on the coffee.

"Dad, I didn't mean that."

Janet stopped in midstep. Reese was with his father and Janet had heard that tone of voice between the two men enough to know that they were arguing. Electricity seemed to hang in the air. Janet could feel it even from this distance.

"I know you didn't, son." The elder man sounded defeated and discouraged. Janet could picture him hunched forward. She had seen him sitting like that in the past and had wondered what painful memories haunted him. The cheerful facade had never reached his eyes. There was an ache in Samuel Edwards' life, one that went deep enough to reach his soul.

"Reese, you're wasting your life. You can't fool me, I see the restlessness in you. I want you to be happy. Why do you insist on dating these blondes? Do you want this Bubbles girl to mother my grandchildren?" the older man questioned, his voice vaguely pleading.

"Bunny," Reese corrected sharply.

"Bubbles, Bunny, I don't see the difference. Why is it you can't be serious with nice girls?"

"Dad." Again Reese's voice was filled with warning.

"A girl like Janet."

"I think I've had enough of this conversation."

Although Janet couldn't see the two men, she could tell from the direction of Reese's voice that he had moved to the other side of the office.

"Why is it you never want to discuss Janet?" Samuel Edwards demanded. "The last time I suggested you marry Janet you nearly threw me out of my own office."

Enough, Janet's mind screamed . . . enough. Wildly she looked around her like a trapped animal seeking escape. Making as little noise as possible, she walked out of the office.

Chapter Eight

"Janet, can I talk to you a minute."

Janet wiped her hands on the terry-cloth apron tied around her waist. "Sure, Dad."

Stewart Montgomery's eyes were guarded as Janet approached. Sundays after the church service she usually joined her parents for the main meal of the day. Janet had felt her father studying her and had done her best to disguise her unhappiness. But few things slipped past her father.

"Sit down, princess."

With a weak smile, Janet sat on the arm of his chair and looped her hand around his shoulder. The fingers of the other hand toyed with the thick dark hair streaked with gray. There seemed to be a lot more gray lately. Lovingly she placed her cheek on top of his head and sighed unevenly.

"You were never very good at hiding things. From the time you were a little girl your mother and I knew whenever something was bothering you."

Her laugh was filled with the memories of a girlhood long past. "I know."

"Something's been bothering you for weeks now," her father continued. "When you came for Joel on Thursday you were irritated and restless. And today it's no better." He paused and patted her hand. "Usually I like to stay out of your life, let you handle your own affairs, but something's wrong and has been for several months. I hesitate to say anything, but I'm more than your father, I'm your spiritual leader too. Can you tell me what's happened to make you so unhappy?"

Janet glanced into the kitchen to see her mother entertaining Joel and realized that her parents had planned this. Her mother was obviously keeping Joel busy so Janet and her father wouldn't be disturbed.

Softly she smiled to herself. "I'm in love."

"Reese Edwards?"

Janet swallowed back the surprise. Had she been so easy to read? "Yes," she mumbled. "How'd you know?"

His hard shoulders raised and lowered with a gentle shrug. "I think both your mother and I guessed as much the time Reese brought you and Joel home from the movie, several months back."

167

Janet's mouth opened to object, then closed as the lie refused to form. "Yes, I loved him then."

"He doesn't love you?" The question was issued thoughtfully.

"I don't know, I don't think so . . . Oh, Dad, it's all so confusing. Reese Edwards is a man of the world, his women are . . ." She searched desperately for the right word.

"Worldly?" her father interjected.

"Blonde and beautiful and so stereotyped it's almost unreal. Reese's interest in me is only fleeting; he's attracted to me, but the attraction seems to be . . ." Again she hesitated.

"Physical."

Janet nodded, because verbally confirming his conclusion was painful and embarrassing.

"Have you thought about changing jobs?"

"A thousand times," she said, her words emphatic. "I've typed up my resignation so often I've lost count. But when the opportunity comes to give it to him, I can't. I just can't do it." Her sigh was bittersweet. "It's worth the emotional upheaval to be close to him. For now I can live with that."

"He continues to date his blondes."

"Oh yes. This current one has lasted longer than any."

Her father didn't make any comment.

"Dad." Janet drew in a deep breath to steady her trembling voice. "I know this sounds crazy, but I believe the biggest cross I have to bear in my life is *me*. My weaknesses, my temptations, my pride, most especially my pride. Reese came to me last week; I was frightened of what he was going to suggest. Frightened that my love for him would make me weak. I was purposely evasive and hurtful. I even went so low as to pretend I was dating another man."

Twisting his position so that Janet was cradled in his arms, Stewart Montgomery tenderly kissed her temple. "I have no pearls of wisdom for you, princess. My love for you is a small thing compared to Christ's love. I can only promise to pray that God will give you wisdom and guide you."

She rested her head on her father's shoulder just as she'd done as a little girl. Comfort, peace and a deep abiding sense of well-being soothed the ache from her heart and cleared her mind.

Reese was out of the office until noon Monday. Janet was preparing to leave for lunch when he strode into the room and paused at her desk to pick up the stack of phone messages.

"Good morning, Miss Montgomery," he greeted without looking at her.

"Good morning, Mr. Edwards."

"Phone Benson's and have the usual piece of jewelry sent to Bunny Jacobs." The order was issued crisply, without emotion.

For a crazy second Janet's heart stopped, then

leaped wildly to her throat. Reese was through with Bunny! It was over, finished. He was casting Bunny from his life as indifferently as he'd toss a used memo in the trash. As always, Janet experienced a sense of outrage. One would think that after all these months of working with Reese she would have become accustomed to his dealings with women. Even though she was jealous of Bunny, she couldn't prevent the feelings of sympathy.

A prayer of appreciation formed on her lips. Thank God she had never revealed her love to Reese. Many times she'd had to bite back the words that seemed to swell from her heart. If she had revealed her feelings, her fate would be no different from that of his latest blonde, left with a broken heart and a piece of jewelry. For a minute Janet could almost hate him.

Her attitude didn't improve during lunch, and afterward her fingers hit the computer keys with unnecessary force as she typed up a report for Reese.

"Is something the matter, Miss Montgomery?" he questioned later.

Her head was turned deliberately away from him. "Nothing," she replied in a controlled tone.

He lingered at her desk, not speaking. The longer Reese remained, the more disturbing his presence became, her nerves taut, pulling. Finally she could endure it no longer.

"Was there something else?" she asked with what she hoped sounded like professional indifference.

Reese looked surprised by the antagonism in her eyes. "Nothing." He pivoted and returned to his portion of the office.

Bunny phoned later that afternoon, sniffling to hold back the wall of tears. "Miss Montgomery," she pleaded. "I know you're not supposed to let me speak to Reese, but could you please put me through? I promise I won't keep him long. I just need to talk to him for a few minutes."

"Of course you can, Miss Jacobs." Without hesitation Janet punched the call through.

Some time later Reese stormed into her office. "What's going on? You knew darn well I didn't want to talk to Bunny."

Janet made busywork straightening her desk, anything to hide the telltale shake of her hands. "If you'll excuse me for saying so, dealing with your hysterical females is not part of my job. It certainly wasn't in my job description."

Reese slammed his fist against the oak desk and Janet's hand flew to her breast as she gave a cry of alarm.

"Your job, Miss Montgomery," Reese ground out between clenched teeth, "is what I tell you, when I tell you and how I tell you. Is that understood?"

The desire to stand, click her heels and salute

him was strong. Her whole body seemed to quiver with resistance, but she forced her unflinching gaze to meet his. "Yes, sir." The words were issued in a tight jeering whisper.

For a minute it looked as if Reese was going to say something more. Anger flashed across his face. In the past Janet had seen Reese angry on several occasions, but never seething like this.

Long after Reese had returned to his office, Janet sat still, her hands clenched in her lap, unable to work. Was this what their relationship had come to? A contest of wills in which Reese was sure to win?

Twenty minutes later he returned. Immediately an uncomfortable silence settled over the room.

"Janet." The use of her first name surprised her. Reese had been stiff and formal since the night he left her apartment two weeks ago.

"Yes?" She reached for her pencil and pad.

Before he crossed his arms in front of his broad chest, he smoothed the hair at the side of his head. "You're right. It's unfair to leave you to deal with the personal aspects of my life." Although issued grudgingly, the apology had nonetheless been made.

For an instant Janet was sure she had misunderstood him. She couldn't believe what she was hearing. Reese was actually saying he was wrong? It seemed impossible. To hide her shock, Janet stood and walked over to the coffeepot and poured herself a cup. She raised the glass pot in mute question and after his curt nod poured him a cup too.

"Well?" His level gaze followed her movements.

She bowed her head, surrounding the Styrofoam cup with both hands. "Thank you, Reese. I know how difficult it was for you to admit that."

He moved beside her and the impact of having him so close was physically unnerving.

"Friends?" he murmured.

Janet's gaze was drawn to him as if by magnetic force. Her smile wavered as she nodded.

"Good." He seemed to relax. "Since that's out of the way, I'd like for you to have dinner with me tonight."

"No!" Her voice shook treacherously.

Reese's disgusted sound of exasperation followed. "Why not?"

"Why not?" She echoed his words. "Tell me, Reese, who's going to order the jewelry when you're done with me?"

"It's different with you," he spoke sharply.

"Of course it is. I know you, I know the games you play," she shot back. "I'm not going to be satisfied with three months and a gold bracelet that says you'll never forget me."

Her words produced a glower of harsh amusement in the dark eyes. He appeared controlled and unaffected by the tension that shook Janet. "I want more too. A whole lot more."

She backed away from him. "This isn't going to work, Reese Edwards, so don't try to sweet-talk me."

A muscle in his lean jaw twitched and, to Janet's dismay, she saw that it was from amusement. The last thing she wanted to do was to entertain him.

"What's so funny?" she demanded, hands resting challengingly on her hips.

"Nothing," he denied with a poor attempt to conceal a smile. "It's just been a long time since I've heard the expression 'sweet talk.' "

Quickly Janet returned to her desk. "If you'll excuse me," she murmured tightly, "I have work to do."

Somehow Janet made it through the remainder of the week. Reese didn't repeat his dinner offer, and if he had, Janet wasn't sure she would have refused. Business was business, but several times she happened to catch Reese watching her movements, studying her, his look unreadable. Janet's heart would scream with frustration. This was all a cat-and-mouse game with him; she was just another challenge.

Unexpectedly Reese gave her Thursday afternoon off, explaining that things were slow and if she wanted extra time with her brother she could have it. Her mind filled with unspoken questions, Janet returned to her apartment.

Friday proved even more unsettling. Reese was on the phone early that morning with an overseas call. Janet could hear him shuffling through the mess that cluttered his desk, searching for something. Past experience had told her to come to the rescue and quick. With a polite tap she opened the communicating door and stuck her head inside, half expecting him to storm at her.

"Do you need something?" she questioned.

Reese looked up, surprised, relief flooding the handsome features. "I can't find the Cummings file. Have you seen it?"

Janet had placed it on his desk the day before and without hesitation sorted through the disorganized piles until she had located the one he needed. She handed it to him and, to her dismay, he leaned over and casually brushed her cheek with his lips. A warm sensation crept over her face, invading her features with burning color. A hand flew to her cheek as if to wipe it away.

Reese's eyes were sparkling and his secret smile was meant for her alone.

Saturday Janet spent the afternoon shopping for material for bridesmaid dresses with Gail. The wedding wasn't for another four months, but Janet was going to sew her own dress and wanted to get an early start. They also stopped at the printer, the jeweler and saw to several other details necessary for the wedding. Janet had never realized how complicated a wedding could be, and although she enjoyed the day she was exhausted. Gail and Ben insisted on taking her out to dinner that night and it was after midnight before she got to bed.

The alarm rang for church early Sunday morning and Janet rolled over and groaned, half tempted to stay in bed. Her attention waned during Sunday school and she read over the bulletin. The volleyball team was starting up again. She wasn't much of an athlete, but she did enjoy playing on the church team, where spirit, not skill, was the most important prerequisite. Placing the announcement in the flap of her Bible, she returned her attention to the lesson.

The front pews were crowded when she entered the main part of the church for the morning worship service. Janet took a seat toward the back. Sitting with her head bowed and her eyes closed, she mentally prepared herself for the coming message. She felt someone enter the pew and sit next to her. Finishing her prayer, she slowly raised her head, half turning to greet the newcomer. The smile died on her lips as she saw it was Reese.

Cordial, as if they were strangers, he nodded in greeting, opened the bulletin and began reading. A Bible, obviously new, rested in his lap. When he finished reading the bulletin he opened the Bible and searched through the table of contents to find Ephesians, the text her father was preaching from that morning.

The worship service wasn't scheduled to begin for several minutes and the strain of sitting beside Reese, maintaining a fragile control of her composure, made Janet want to seek another pew.

As the worship service started, the congregation stood to sing the opening hymn. Reese flipped through the unfamiliar pages of the hymnal, apparently not knowing what song to sing. Janet handed him the open songbook and took his, deftly turning the pages until she located the correct song.

Reese mumbled something under his breath that Janet couldn't hear, but when their gazes met, his mouth was quirked humorously. Without meaning to, Janet responded to the potent warmth of his smile.

The opening song was followed by the morning prayer and a review of the events of the following week. Stewart Montgomery's smile reached across the congregation to rest on Janet.

"Would you like to introduce your guest, Janet?" he asked her.

Reluctantly she stood, her mouth pinched. "Stand up," she whispered under her breath to Reese.

He complied and placed a possessive arm across her shoulder.

"Remove your hand," she hissed behind a phony smile with her teeth clenched.

Instead of doing as she requested, Reese molded a large hand over her shoulder, bringing her even closer to his side. Every cell of her body cried out with the effects of his nearness and when she spoke her voice shook slightly.

"This is Reese Edwards," she introduced him to the congregation, which had centered its attention on her and Reese. "He works for Dyna-Flow too." Quickly she resumed the sitting position, effectively breaking his hold on her.

Several knowing smiles and gentle nods followed as the people sitting around them turned to show their approval.

Janet didn't digest a word of the morning message. Normally she took notes during the sermon, but she was all too conscious of Reese's disturbing presence. She seemed incapable of constructing a coherent sentence, let alone transferring the thought to paper.

Together they stood for the closing hymn. Reese's deep baritone voice rang out with hers. The song was an old familiar one that Reese obviously recognized. Janet was surprised by the rich quality of his singing voice and soon discovered she enjoyed listening to him more than singing herself.

A low murmur filled the church as the congregation stood and began to file out of the building. Janet turned to find that Reese's gaze was centered disturbingly on her.

"Just a Dyna-Flow employee?" he whispered mockingly.

"I didn't want to intimidate anyone," she returned in a polite voice, clenching her Bible to her breast as if it would afford her protection.

"Mr. Reese," Joel called as he flew down the outside church aisle. "Hi, Mr. Reese." He stood breathless and panting.

"Hello, Joel, it's good to see you again," Reese greeted warmly, extending his hand for the youth to shake.

Pleased with the opportunity, Joel pumped Reese's hand with excitement and enthusiasm. "I've been missing you."

"I've missed you too. But I really think that's your sister's fault. We'll have to talk to her, won't we?" Reese looked back to Janet, one brow arched slightly.

"Janny, I like Mr. Reese. I like him a lot. I think you should marry him so I can have a brother-in-law."

Janet could feel the hot flush of color seep up from her neck. "Joel, stop it!" Her voice was harsher than what she intended and tears welled in her brother's eyes.

Reese placed a comforting hand on the youth's shoulder. "I think we're embarrassing your sister." He leaned forward and whispered something in Joel's ear that made the boy grin from ear to ear.

"Can I tell my dad?" Joel questioned eagerly.

179

Reese seemed to give the question thorough consideration, his thumb rubbing the side of his lean, masculine jaw. "No, I think it should be a surprise."

Without question Joel accepted Reese's words. "Did you like coming to church? Can we go to your cabin again soon?" He asked both questions in one breath without pausing between.

Reese chuckled. "Yes to both."

At the mention of the cabin Janet bristled. Was he going to persist in this lie? Pretense, fabrication, distorting the truth—these were things she would be forced to accept with a man like Reese Edwards. How could she love a man like this? she asked herself. How could she care so deeply about this man when it was tearing her apart?

The church had all but emptied by the time they neared the exit. Stewart Montgomery, dressed in a black robe, shook Reese's hand. "Good to see you again, Reese."

"It's good to be here. I enjoyed the sermon, but there are a couple of things I'd like to ask you about later if you have the time."

"Of course I do."

"Mr. Reese is here to learn about faith," Joel explained.

An arm draped over his son's shoulder, Stewart smiled. "We all are."

Janet made a polite excuse and hurried to the parsonage to help her mother with dinner.

Leonora was busy whipping mashed potatoes when Janet came in the back door. "I'll do the salad," she volunteered, laying her purse and Bible on the kitchen table.

"What a pleasant surprise to see your Mr. Edwards again." Her mother paused, pushing a stray white hair off her weathered forehead.

"He's not mine, Mother," Janet corrected stiffly. "He's not anyone's, and I sincerely doubt that he ever will be."

Her mother blinked, then smiled. "Oh, I doubt that, Janet. A man just needs the right kind of girl, that's all."

Joel burst in the back door, nearly taking the door off the hinges. "Dad and Mr. Reese are talking real serious." Before anyone could stop him, he flew out the door again.

Janet couldn't help feeling cynical. Would Reese stoop so low as to pretend an interest in Christ in an effort to get her? The suspicious thought immediately filled her with shame. Shouldn't she give him the benefit of the doubt?

Ten minutes later Joel burst into the room again. "Dad invited Mr. Reese to dinner," he announced breathlessly.

"Stay in, young man," Leonora insisted.

"Ah, Mom." He stomped his foot and cast a longing glance over his shoulder.

"Close the door and set the table," she continued

181

in a soft voice that both siblings recognized as unswerving.

With a muttered grumble, Joel complied, bringing down the Sunday plates and setting them on the mahogany table in the dining room.

The roast beef, peas, mashed potatoes and gravy were dished into serving bowls and steaming when Reese and Janet's father entered the house.

Brushing the hair away from her face, Leonora Montgomery extended a hand to Reese. "Welcome to our home."

Janet stood awkwardly in the background as the greetings were exchanged. She hovered uncertainly for a minute until she saw where her mother was seating Reese, hoping she could avoid sitting beside him. Luckily Joel was appointed the privilege.

As always, the family joined hands for grace. Her hands linked with her mother's and father's, Janet bowed her head for the short prayer, but when she raised her eyes she found them captured by Reese's. Quickly her lashes fluttered downward as she struggled to conceal the effect his look had upon her senses.

Janet didn't speak unless a question was directed to her. She wasn't uncomfortable with Reese in her family home—not like she'd been the first time—but her feelings were jumbled and confused.

Afterward she stayed in the kitchen, helping her

mother with the dishes. Snatches of the conversation between Reese and her father drifted into the room where the two women were working. Her father seemed to be giving Reese some reading material. At one point she heard him comment, "You'll have to get that book from Janet."

Deliberately she left before Reese did, claiming she had some things that needed to be finished at home. Her father eyed her suspiciously as she made her excuses.

"Childish." She spoke the word out loud. There wasn't another word to describe her behavior. Her car was parked in the church parking lot and Janet paused, wrapping her coat more securely around her as she looked at the church building.

Releasing a long, uneven breath, Janet walked toward the back door. It remained unlocked. Without conscious direction she walked past the Sunday school classrooms, through the foyer to the sanctuary. For a minute she stood at the back of the church, her wildly beating heart sounding in her ears. Why was she here? What had driven her back into the building? Without self-directing thought she took a step forward, then another until she stood before the altar. Slowly she went to her knees.

"Oh, Father," she prayed silently, "I love him." Janet wasn't sure how long she had knelt and prayed, pouring out her heart and her love. She offered up Reese and the love she had concealed from her boss all these months. The words seemed to pour out of her, all the hurt, the doubts, the questions.

When she stood her knees felt shaky. A soft smile lifted the corners of her mouth as she took a step in retreat, her heart and mind cleansed.

Gail was with Ben at his parents' house for the day, and Janet unlocked the apartment door feeling a little lost, and a little lonely. Placing her Bible on the end table, she slipped off her pumps and walked with bare feet into the kitchen to put on hot water. Once the teakettle was filled and on the burner, she unbuttoned her coat and took out a hanger from the hall closet.

When the doorbell rang, her pulse jerked in her throat. She didn't need to open the door to know it was Reese. Somehow she had known he would follow her home. She hurried and hung up her coat and slipped on her shoes. Even with shoes she was at a disadvantage. The doorbell chimed again before she opened the door.

"Hello, Janet."

"Reese." She stepped aside, letting him in. Hands behind her back, she leaned against the door as it closed. The door made a loud clicking sound as it shut, gently rocking her shoulders.

"I imagine you're here to collect that book Dad was telling you about," she said, striving to sound informal. "If you tell me which one it is I'll be glad to get it for you."

His gaze was disturbing and intense as it swept over her. "It was C. S. Lewis' *Mere Christianity*."

Swiftly she lowered her gaze. "It's in my room. I'll only be a minute." It didn't take her long to retrieve it from the small bookcase on the headboard of her bed.

Reese was standing in the same place when she returned. His shoulders were hunched forward slightly and he looked uncomfortable, uneasy.

The teakettle whistled and Janet handed him the book before swiftly walking past him and into the kitchen. Reese followed her.

"Would you like a cup?" she asked, her back to him.

"You know what I want." The words were issued in a husky whisper as his hands closed over her shoulders and turned her around.

Pliantly Janet slipped her arms around his neck and tilted her head back, inviting the exploration of her mouth.

Like a hawk swooping down upon its prey, Reese captured her mouth, kissing her until she was breathless and weak with longing.

"Oh, Reese," she whispered, burying her face in the thick of his sweater.

His hands molded her against the length of his body as he inhaled deep, uneven breaths, as if to gain control of himself. His chin moved back and forth on top of her head in a slow sensuous movement, mussing her hair.

"I think we're both crazy," Janet stammered.

Reese didn't speak immediately and when he did, his voice was husky and tight. "You've been driving me crazy for months."

"You shouldn't have come here today." She drew in a shaky breath.

Gently Reese kissed her temple. "I couldn't stay away any longer. I don't want to rush you. I want everything to be right between us."

Janet nodded, her hands roaming over his back, enjoying the feel of his sweater and the taut muscles beneath her palms.

"I want you to come up to the cabin with me," he whispered in her ear, lifting the soft curls away from her shoulder so he could kiss the slim column of her neck.

Janet felt the blood drain out of her face. Roughly she pulled herself free of his embrace and backed away.

A puzzled look marred his features. "What's wrong? What'd I say?" His expression softened and his bewilderment was replaced with a knowing look. "Janet, nothing's going to happen. I won't let it, I promise."

Her arms hugging her middle, she shook her head. "The day you didn't show up for work, I . . . I thought you might be at the cabin . . ."

Reese jerked his fingers through his hair. "I was."

The acid burn of forming tears stung her eyes

and she swiveled around and moved into the living room.

"Janet, what is it?"

To keep the humiliating tears from falling, Janet lifted her face and stared at the ceiling. "I . . . I was worried sick. I didn't know where you could be and when I spoke to your father and suggested that you could be there, he told me you didn't have a cabin." She swung around, angry. "That whole beautiful day we spent there was a lie, a farce, and you're doing it again." She lifted balled fists from her side as if to strike him. "For once, just once, be honest with me."

"Janet, listen." He moved in front of her and placed both hands over her shoulders, but when she jerked herself free he dropped his arms to his side. "I didn't lie to you. As far as I know, I've never lied to you. The cabin is mine. I've owned it for two years. I've considered it my private escape from the pressures of my job. I've never told anyone about it, or taken anyone there but you and your brother." The lack of emotion in his voice made everything all the more believable.

"No one?" Janet questioned softly, desperately needing assurance.

"Only you," he repeated.

Long brown curls fell forward as she buried her chin in her shoulder. "I've been such a fool," she mumbled.

A hand gently caressed her cheek before sliding

beneath her hair and drawing her into his arms.

Willingly Janet complied, cupping his head with her hands so she could rain kisses over every part of his face. Gently her lips pressed fleeting kisses over his eyes, his cheek, his chin, his throat until, with a deep groan, Reese took command, burying his fingers in her hair and directing her mouth to his.

She had battled this attraction for so long that she was devoid of the willpower to deny it any longer. She moaned softly in surrender as his mouth parted hers. Every sense was filled with Reese, lost in a vortex of undeniable longing.

It was Reese who pulled away, taking deep ragged breaths as he buried his face in her neck. "I think you'd better fix me some coffee."

Weakly Janet nodded, delaying as long as possible leaving his arms. Her hands slid from his back to his chest, reveling in the feel of the steel-hard muscles beneath the thick sweater. Tilting her head back, she smiled into his sea blue eyes. The temptation was to slip her arms around his neck and bring his mouth back to hers, but she resisted. It was chilly outside the protective circle of his arms.

"You have a wonderful family," Reese commented as he lowered his six-foot frame onto a kitchen chair.

"I think your dad is great myself."

Janet caught his expression before he could

disguise it. Suddenly her stomach lurched sickeningly as a new thought dawned on her. Reese didn't want her; this was all an act to satisfy his father. Hadn't she heard Samuel Edwards pleading with Reese to date a girl like herself?

"You'd do anything for Sam, wouldn't you?"

Reese glanced at her curiously. "Just about."

Steeling herself, Janet backed against the kitchen counter for support. "Including ditching Bunny and dating a nice girl," she swallowed tightly. "A nice girl like Janet."

The chair made a hard sound against the floor as he stood. "It's not what you're thinking."

Janet closed her eyes as the waves of agony washed over her. "I thought you said you've never lied to me."

Chapter Nine

Janet arrived at the office an hour early Monday morning. She'd typed the letter of resignation so many times that her fingers flew across the keys without thought. As the paper reeled off the printer, she reread the words. It sounded so cold, so cut and dried, as if two years of her life could be blotted out with only a few carefully chosen words printed on a plain piece of paper. The black ink seemed to glare back at her from the white paper. Black and white. The contrast seemed to represent her relationship with Reese. The words blurred for a moment as her eyes refused to focus. Janet and Reese were too different, like trying to mix oil and water. She had been a fool to believe Reese would ever change. But not anymore. Not after today.

Brisk steps carried her into his office and she placed the letter on the desk where it would receive his prompt attention. It stated that in lieu of two weeks' notice she would be taking the vacation due her, effective immediately.

It wasn't long before she had removed the personal items from her desk and the room. When everything was neatly placed in a small box she had brought with her, Janet phoned the employment service Reese had used in the past and set up interviews to begin that afternoon. Another quick call brought a substitute from the steno pool to take her place.

All that was left was to wait for her replacement. Janet had hoped to be gone before Reese arrived, but he walked in the door twenty minutes ahead of schedule.

"I want to talk to you," he demanded in an iron voice that wouldn't easily be defied.

Janet bolted upright, pausing to push her glasses from the tip of her nose. "Good morning, Mr. Edwards." Her voice was heavy with sarcastic undertones.

A punishing grip on her upper arm forced her into his office. "I said I wanted to talk to you," he repeated, his eyes hardening into chips of blue ice.

Janet yanked her arm free. "Don't touch me."

"I'll do more than touch you if you don't listen to reason," he said harshly.

Janet chose to ignore him, instead taking the letter of resignation from his desk and handing it to him. "I believe you'll find everything in order. I've called the employment agency and set up interviews. The appointment times are on my desk. Also, Mary Kaufman from the steno pool will be replacing me until you hire a new secretary." She strived to keep her voice level and businesslike.

"You can't resign," Reese argued. "You owe me two weeks' notice."

"If you'll read my letter you'll find that I'm taking the vacation due me instead."

The anger and frustration seemed to boil within him as he paced the floor in front of her. "Janet, don't do this."

She gave him a wary glance. There was a faint pleading quality to his voice so unlike the man that she thought she knew. Sadly Janet lowered her head and gave it a short shake. "I won't reconsider."

"If you'd only listen to me I could—"

"No," she interrupted hoarsely, "there's nothing more you can say. I heard it all yesterday. I don't want to listen anymore." Her lips trembled and she bit into the soft inner flesh of her cheek to hide the telltale quiver. "I refuse to work for a man I neither respect nor like."

Reese inhaled a long, hard breath.

A polite knock at his office door centered their attention on the young girl who had entered the room.

"Good morning, Janet." She smiled, oblivious to the tension that arced like warring bolts of electricity around the room. "Did you call for me?"

"Yes . . . yes I did."

"Get out," Reese stormed.

Ignoring his outrage, Janet looked at the girl calmly. "I'll be with you in a minute, Mary. Wait for me in the other room."

Mary's face was tight and unsure, but she did as she was asked, quietly closing the door.

"I don't believe there's anything more to be said."

"Janet." A wealth of emotion seemed to burst from Reese as he called her name.

She couldn't trust him. Regret rippled over her and for an instant she closed her eyes. Even after everything she knew about him, the desire to stay, to be with him was so strong it almost overcame her. With her chin tilted at a proud angle, Janet walked out the office and didn't look back.

It felt strange to be home on a Monday morning.

The apartment looked cold and empty. The minute she walked in, it was a battle not to phone the office and review things with Mary one more time. Certainly there was something she'd forgotten. "It's not your responsibility anymore," she told herself aloud.

Janet sat at the kitchen table with a cup of coffee. Her feet were propped on the chair opposite hers. The classified section of the newspaper was spread across the surface of the table. Janet forced herself to read through the columns of jobs listed, mentally finding fault with each one.

When she could endure it no longer, Janet phoned Reese's office at a time she knew he would be in a meeting.

"How's it going?" she asked Mary in a feigned carefree voice.

"Fine," Mary told her, but she sounded strained.

"Well." Janet hesitated. "If you have any questions, I'll be here the rest of the day; feel free to phone me. Do you have my number?"

"I don't think I'd better. Mr. Edwards made it clear that I'm not supposed to contact you in any way. No one is."

"Oh." She couldn't restrain the small shocked sound. It hadn't taken Reese long to completely sever her ties with Dyna-Flow.

"Thanks for calling anyway," Mary said softly in sympathy. "So far everything's running pretty smoothly. Other than warning me that I'm not to have any contact with you, Mr. Edwards has been nice. Oh, by the way, I heard him call the accounting office to have your check mailed to you."

"That . . . that was thoughtful of him. I'm sure everything will be fine. Good-bye, Mary."

"Good-bye."

Fingers clenching the receiver, Janet slowly replaced it in its cradle. Reese didn't need her. Within minutes after she'd left he had effectively cast her from his life. She wasn't any different from one of his blondes. Cheaper. This time he didn't have to pay for a bracelet.

By the time Gail walked in the door that evening, Janet had two interviews scheduled for later in the week.

"You really did it, didn't you?" Gail hung her coat in the hall closet and kicked off her shoes, walking barefoot into the kitchen, where Janet was busy frying hamburger.

"Yup, I did."

Gail flopped into a chair. "Any regrets?"

Hoping to relate an indifferent, untroubled impression, she shrugged her shoulders and gave unnecessary attention to stirring the frying meat. "Not a one."

"You're not likely to find a job that pays as well."

"I know. But some things aren't worth money." Like being hopelessly in love with her boss, she silently reminded herself. "It seems I've been deluding myself with my importance. I talked to Mary this afternoon and everything was fine."

"Don't be so hasty," Gail said thoughtfully. "I don't think anyone, especially Reese, knew or appreciated all you did to keep the office running smoothly."

Janet remembered a time when Reese had told her how much he needed her, appreciated her handling of his affairs. That had been months ago. Now Janet was sure that he would do anything rather than admit that.

The next afternoon Gail entered the house, a knowing smile lighting her eyes. "Mary left Mr. Edwards' office crying this afternoon. She refuses to work for him another minute. Steno sent up a replacement," she announced casually.

"What happened?" Conflicting emotions crowded Janet's mind. Perhaps she'd forgotten to tell Mary something and the incident had been her fault. But there was also a small feeling of triumph.

Janet's interview with a downtown brokerage firm didn't go well the next morning. When the interviewer questioned her reasons for leaving Dyna-Flow, Janet stammered and looked away uneasily. "I'm looking for a change of pace," she said finally, but she noted that the interviewer's attitude changed sharply afterward. Janet didn't need to be told she was out of the running for that job.

Janet picked up Joel early Thursday afternoon.

"Hi, Janny." He met her at the front door. "What are we going to do today?"

Before Janet could answer she saw the book resting on the dining room table. The front cover seemed to glare at her, blinding her vision. C. S. Lewis' *Mere Christianity*, the book Reese had borrowed last Sunday.

"Janny, where are we going?" Joel demanded impatiently.

Janet looked to him with a blank expression on her face. "I'm sorry, Joel. What did you say?"

Friday morning Janet returned to the apartment after another interview. She hadn't done much better with this one. Defeated, she tossed her jacket on the back of the worn couch and walked into the kitchen to get the newspaper. Maybe it was time to make a complete change in her life. Try something new and different like . . . She opened the paper to the classified section and read the first ad that caught her eye. A plumber. That's it; she'd become a plumber.

The doorbell chimed and Janet jerked around, surprised. A glance in the peephole showed it was Reese's father.

"Mr. Edwards." She tried to hide her surprise as she opened the door for him.

"Hello, Janet." His eyes were tired, but kind.

"Come in, please."

He followed her inside and sat on the couch. Self-consciously, Janet removed her jacket and hung it in the closet.

"What can I do for you?" She remained standing, hands clenched tightly in front of her.

The elder man leaned forward until his elbows rested on his knees. Janet couldn't prevent the small smile that touched her soft mouth. Many times Reese sat in exactly the same way and Janet couldn't hold back a flood of sadness.

"My son has gone through four secretaries in as many days." Samuel Edwards ignored her question.

Janet's mouth tightened. "I'm sorry to hear that."

"He needs you, but he won't ask you to come back." He seemed to be studying Janet closely.

"I'm aware of that." She tucked a stray curl behind her ear. Pride wouldn't allow Reese to admit he needed anyone or anything.

"Reese won't ask you, but I will. Janet, for the sanity of the whole company, will you please come back?"

"No." Arms hugging her waist, she turned and walked to the other side of the room. "I can't," she said with less conviction. Her hand made a weak, sweeping gesture.

"Why not?"

"I just can't." To her horror, her voice cracked and she struggled for a moment to regain her composure. "I'm sorry Reese is having trouble finding a replacement, but my returning would be impossible." She had to force herself to speak.

"If you could come back and work out the two weeks' notice. At least then there would be ample time for Reese to hire and train someone else."

Janet hesitated, the temptation strong to do as he asked. "All right," she agreed. "But only until a suitable replacement can be trained, and not a minute longer."

Immediately the dull eyes brightened. "Wonderful." He sat upright and clapped his hands. Cocking his head at an angle, he paused. "Maybe it would be better if we didn't mention my visit to Reese. No need to stir up a storm of indignation."

Janet laughed. "I agree. When do you want me?"

"Is this afternoon too soon?" he asked as he stood. "From what I hear, Reese threw out the latest girl by nine-thirty this morning. No one from steno will work for him and the agency couldn't send in anyone else until Monday."

Janet expelled her breath on a long sigh. Maybe it would be best to meet the lion in his lair now and avoid fretting over the confrontation over the weekend. "I'll be there within the hour."

Samuel Edwards nodded approvingly. "Thank you, Janet."

Thirty minutes later, Janet sauntered into Dyna-

Flow. A hush fell over the floor as she walked out of the elevator. Lenny Forrestal ran to greet her, fell to his knees and kissed the hem of her skirt.

"Are you coming back?" he pleaded, his hands folded as if in prayer. "Please, please tell me it's true."

Irritably, Janet glanced down at him. "Cut it out, Lenny."

"Are you back for good?" someone Janet didn't recognize called out to her.

It was better to set the record straight now. "No," she explained in a crisp voice. "Only until someone else is trained."

The murmuring sound of everyone speaking at once followed her down the corridor until she reached Reese's office. Janet gasped as she opened the door. Her cabinet drawers were open and files scattered over the carpet. Her desk was a mess of papers and reports. It looked as if someone had splashed coffee over the contents of the entire desk.

Incensed, Janet briskly walked around the mess and knocked on Reese's door.

"Go away."

Ignoring his bad mood, Janet twisted the doorknob and stormed inside. Hands resting on her hips, her eyes flashing, Janet glared at him indignantly. "I'm not even gone five days and this whole office looks like a pigpen. What's going on?"

Reese leaped out of his high-backed leather chair. "What are you doing here?" he demanded fiercely.

As quickly as it had risen, the anger drained out of her. "I've reconsidered. It was unfair to leave you in the lurch. I'll work out my two weeks' notice and train my replacement. It's only fair."

His mouth moved into a crooked, jeering line. "Don't do me any favors, Miss Montgomery. You've made your position clear."

She pivoted sharply. "Make sure it remains clear." Without another word she closed the door and set about straightening the mess in the outer room.

At five o'clock Samuel Edwards stepped into the office and gave Janet a conspiratorial wink. "Why, Janet, you're back. What a pleasant surprise. I hope you'll stay. Is Reese available?" He spoke in an unusually loud voice, apparently wanting his son to overhear the conversation.

Janet returned the wink and smiled. "Go in." The door remained open a crack and Janet couldn't help hearing the conversation. To close it would only call attention to herself.

"I see Janet's back."

"You old goat. You asked her to, didn't you?" Reese accused.

"Me?" came Samuel Edwards' shocked reply.

"There's irony in this situation, isn't there, Dad?" Reese was using the same contemptuous tone he'd used earlier with her. "You can ask my secretary, who means nothing to you, to come back, but not my mother, who meant everything to me."

Janet heard the sharply inhaled breath that betrayed deep pain. A second later, his shoulders hunched, Samuel Edwards walked out of the office.

Stunned, Janet stared after him. Never had she seen a man look more broken.

A sound exploded from the other room as if Reese had thrown something against the wall. Janet jumped at the unexpected noise. A moment later the office door was jerked open as Reese flew out of the room. He hesitated in the doorway before calling his father.

Janet remained where she was standing by the filing cabinets. Several times before she had sensed something was wrong between Reese and his father. Something deep and painful. She looked out the open door, realizing how much she loved these men, both of them. As she closed her eyes a prayer rose automatically from her heart, a petition that whatever hurt was between Reese and his father would be settled and cleared away forever.

Saturday morning Janet decided to return to Dyna-Flow and finish what she hadn't had time for on Friday. The security men knew her well enough to let her in without a problem. She had been working for about an hour when Reese strolled in. He looked surprised to see her; his gaze narrowed fractionally.

Not expecting to see Reese, Janet had worn jeans and a sweater. Rubbing her hands on her thighs, she looked down, self-consciously aware of how the denim fabric molded against her hips and legs.

"Miss Montgomery." The greeting was stilted.

"Good morning, Mr. Edwards." Her voice wasn't any less brittle.

Coffee was ready, and more from tradition than because she was being friendly, Janet took him in a cup a few minutes later. As was his habit, he didn't look up from his work as she placed the cup on his desk.

"Thank you, Janet."

The acknowledgment surprised her. "You're welcome."

Reese paused, wrapping both hands around the pen he was holding, his eyes not meeting hers. "I wasn't referring to the coffee." His head bent down as he resumed scribbling notes across a report he was studying.

For a moment Janet watched him, her heart pounding so loud she was sure he must be able to hear it. Samuel Edwards was right, Reese would never have asked her to come back. And now, she was shocked by his expressed appreciation.

Reese left the office about noon without

speaking to her again. Janet watched him walk out. Yesterday afternoon and this morning had proven that they were capable of working together. Not that it was easy, with tension mounting every minute. Yet along with the emotional pain of being near Reese, Janet felt a crazy sort of contentment. He would never belong to her, and would probably never commit himself to any woman. Time had taught her that. But knowing the type of man he was didn't lessen the love she felt for him.

Love. Janet stopped typing, her hands resting on the keyboard. What a difficult thing love was to understand. With Gail and Ben it had begun as a friendship that had matured, slowly developing as they spent time together. Janet had been shocked when she was forced to acknowledge her feelings for Reese. It had happened suddenly, almost explosively.

She was still tangled in her thoughts when Reese unexpectedly sauntered into the room, carrying two white sacks.

"I thought you might like some lunch."

Woodenly, Janet accepted the sack. "Thank you," she mumbled in a choked voice, astonishment dictating her words and actions.

He entered his office and closed the door. Opening the sack, Janet spread out the napkin and took out the roast beef sandwich, small salad and—she nearly laughed out loud—a huge piece of apple pie. Regret flickered in her blue eyes as she glanced at the closed office door. He ate his lunch alone on the other side, just as she ate hers alone. It was a fitting salute to a relationship that was never meant to be.

Monday morning arrived and everything had returned to normal. It was as if Janet had never left. Reese was in his office when she brought in his mail and morning cup of coffee. He didn't acknowledge her presence.

Janet waited until she had returned to her desk before buzzing him on the intercom.

"Yes." His response was clipped.

"I'll call the employment agency this morning and set up interviews for this afternoon if you agree."

"Fine." The word came back hard and cold.

The first interview was scheduled for early afternoon. Janet introduced herself to the young woman and reviewed the application. She felt guilty when she noted the woman was married and had two children. Reese never had anything to do with married women.

Janet escorted the woman into Reese's office. "Mr. Edwards, this is Pauline Bower."

Reese was already asking pertinent questions when Janet stepped out of the room.

A half hour later Pauline joined Janet. Her face was slightly red.

"How'd it go?" Janet asked pleasantly.

Pauline sighed and shook her head. "Awful, just awful. He asked me to spell some horrible word I've never heard of before. Really weird. He wanted to know the last time I got drunk and what church I attended." She opened her purse and removed Reese's business card and dumped it in the garbage. "As far as I'm concerned your boss can keep this job."

Two interviews were scheduled for the next day. One in the morning and another later that afternoon. Both applicants came out of the meeting with negative looks. Janet didn't have the opportunity to question either of them, but she realized it wasn't going to be easy to find a replacement that would please Reese.

By Friday Janet had paraded several more applicants in and out of his office.

"All right," she told him stiffly, sitting in the chair opposite his desk. "Instead of wasting everyone's time, including yours and mine, let's make up a list of exactly what you want in a secretary."

"Fine." He leaned back in his chair and began to dictate his demands. "I want someone with high organizational skills, computer confidence, the ability to take shorthand and Dictaphone capabilities."

Janet noted the information down on her pad, well aware that every applicant he had seen possessed all of these abilities.

"I'd also like my secretary to have won an

award in spelling, enjoy apple pie and wear glasses that slip down to the tip of her nose when she's taking dictation," he continued.

Janet's thoughts clashed with the force of two mountain goats ramming their heads. Reese was telling her he wanted her. She closed her eyes as a betraying light of love burned deep from within her eyes.

"Mr. Edwards," she said with marked patience. "May I remind you that I will only be here a few more days. If you wish to have me train my replacement, then I believe every effort should be made to hire one."

Reese leaned forward to rest his elbows on his desk. His fingers formed a loose triangle, his index fingers pressed to his mouth. "I agree," he murmured, seeming deep in thought. "I agree wholeheartedly."

With barely restrained irritation, Janet stood and returned to the outer office. After a quick phone call to the employment agency, she cleaned off her desk. Gail would be up to meet her any minute and she didn't wish to stay any longer than necessary tonight.

"Janet"—Gail breathlessly burst into the room—"guess what? No, don't guess. Ben ran into Gary Jensen this afternoon. Ben phoned the office and wants us to meet them after work. Everything's planned. We're going out for Chinese food and to a movie."

"Oh." Janet did her best to hide her lack of enthusiasm.

"Hey, don't look so thrilled."

Janet refused to meet Gail's piercing eyes. "I don't know about you, but it's been a long week. My idea of an exciting evening is to go home, laze in a tub of luscious bubbles and read a good book."

"Janet," Gail pleaded in a hushed voice, warily eyeing the door to Reese's office. "For heaven's sake, you can't pine your life away on him." Her head quirked toward Reese's office.

"I'm not," Janet insisted, her eyes rounding derisively. "Just because I don't feel like fitting into plans you made without consulting me isn't any reason to concern yourself in matters that are none of your business." Her voice increased in volume with every word she spoke until the last phrase was practically shouted.

For a moment Gail looked stunned. Her mouth opened to say something, then closed again.

Janet rubbed her hand over her eyes. Why should she be waspish with the best friend she had in the world? It only proved that working with Reese was becoming increasingly impossible. Perhaps in the back of her mind she was hoping that he wouldn't find a replacement, so she would have an excuse to stay.

"I apologize, Gail. I didn't mean that. A movie does sound like a good idea. And seeing Gary again will be fun." She made every effort to force some enthusiasm into her voice, but she didn't fool her friend, who continued to eye her suspiciously.

Her fingers fumbled as she pulled open the bottom drawer and took out her purse.

"We'll have a good time," Janet said, more to convince herself than from any inner belief. Gary was nice and they had dated several times in the past, but he was so ordinary. There wasn't that spark of excitement that being with Reese— Immediately she forced her thoughts to an abrupt halt. This line of thinking had to cease immediately. She had to stop comparing every man she dated to Reese. Her lungs hurt and Janet realized that she had unconsciously been holding her breath.

Apparently unaware of the tug-of-war going on inside Janet, Gail sighed longingly. "We will have a good time. I think meeting Gary again is just the thing you need to take your mind off of you know who. Gary's always been half in love with you. With the least encouragement I think—" Gail stopped suddenly and stiffened. "Good afternoon, Mr. Edwards."

"Miss Templeton." Reese nodded curtly to Gail, but his eyes swung to Janet, his mouth tightly pressed into an angry line. "Have a nice weekend, Miss Montgomery," he told her stiffly.

"I'm sure I will." Her voice sounded hard with

determination as she stood and walked out the door with Gail. The door remained open and Janet had the unshakable sensation that Reese had moved to the doorway and was watching her move down the long narrow hall that led to the elevator. The nerves at the back of her neck were tingling with awareness. A crazy sense of loyalty, and if she was honest with herself, love, burned within her. She wanted to turn around, run back and assure Reese that Gary meant nothing to her.

"It's better this way," she said without realizing she had spoken aloud.

"Pardon?" Gail glanced over to her.

"Nothing." Janet shook her head, hoping to disguise the sadness she felt must be showing in her eyes.

Sunday morning in church Janet sat with her mother and Joel. She bowed her head to prepare her heart for the coming message.

"Where's Mr. Reese?" Joel leaned over and whispered in her ear.

Janet had no desire to give a long explanation to her brother and chose to ignore his question.

"Janny." He poked her side with his elbow. "Mr. Reese said he'd be coming to church every Sunday. Where is he?" The whispered question was more persistent.

Janet fluttered her lashes open and glanced to her mother, hoping the older woman would recognize Janet's plight and handle the situation. But her mother was busy writing notes on a prayer list she kept in her Bible.

"I don't know, Joel. Reese didn't say anything to me."

"But he did to me," Joel insisted. "He whispered it in my ear. He said that he wanted to learn about Jesus. He said that he was going to come to church on Sundays, he even said—"

"Shush." Janet placed a warning finger across her mouth. "Church is not the place to discuss what Mr. Reese said."

"But, Janny—"

The fiery look she flashed him silenced him immediately.

Joel leaned against the pew, his back straightening. "I won't tell you then," he said and pressed his lips tightly closed. "It was supposed to be a secret anyway."

The next day Reese was scheduled to be out of the office until noon, so Janet made an appointment for an interview the following morning. The woman's qualifications were perfect. The lady from the employment agency assured Janet that there was little to fault in Ms. Christy Karle. After listening to her list of accomplishments and skills, Janet could well understand why she had received such a high recommendation. If Reese found an excuse not to hire Ms. Karle, then Janet would take immediate action herself. His little game of blackmail wasn't going to work. Friday was her last day and it didn't matter how unpleasant Reese was afterward. It wasn't her concern. If the whole company quit on him, then he deserved it.

After sorting the mail, Janet took the items that would need his immediate attention into his office. His desk was in a terrible state. How anyone could work in such mass confusion was beyond her. Since he wasn't due in until noon, Janet decided to straighten the mess. At least then he would be able to see what she had added to the desk. It wouldn't be lost in the stacks of files and reports.

Janet began by clearing the desk and stacking files, reports and cost sheets in neat piles. A caricature caught her by surprise, stopping her movements as she found the likeness of herself staring back at her. Her face had been divided in two. On one half she was smiling, happy, her look angelic, a halo above her head. On the other half her look was cruel and taunting. A devil's horn was projecting from her hair.

Janet stared at the likeness for a long time as the hurt began to grow inside her. Huge tears filled her eyes, thick lashes damming the emotion until one spilled and then another, weaving a crooked path down her suddenly pale cheek. Reese saw her as a hypocrite. The picture proved that he looked upon her relationship with Christ as phony. On one side she was good and on the other, evil.

Her hand was shaking as she raised it to cover her mouth. Slowly her lashes fluttered downward as she struggled not to cry aloud. Nothing had ever hurt so much.

Chapter Ten

The main-floor receptionist buzzed Janet early Tuesday afternoon.

"Christy Karle is here for an interview with Mr. Edwards."

"Thanks, Gladys," Janet said, her body poised yet tense. "Send her up, I'll meet her at the elevator."

"The latest applicant?" Reese questioned, leaning against the wooden doorframe with a lackadaisical expression.

"Yes," she confirmed avoiding his gaze. "She comes highly recommended." She paused, lowering her gaze. "They all have," she added shakily.

"*You* could stay," Reese suggested softly.

Janet was so shocked she glanced up sharply at him. For an instant it was hard to breath as the pain gripped her heart.

"You and I have always worked well together." His voice was dangerously persuasive. "We're a business team."

Janet noted that he qualified the exact nature of their relationship: the office. Unflinching, her eyes met his.

"No!" she replied bitterly. She would be crazy to even consider his suggestions. It was difficult enough to sever her ties with Reese, but the decision had been made easier for her after the discovery of the caricature.

He shrugged, his eyes expressionless, his face a proud mask. It was as if he had made the obligatory offer and her response didn't really matter. "Fine," he said crisply and retreated into his office.

Janet was at the elevator when the metal doors glided open. The lone occupant stepped forward and Janet had to hold her breath to keep from gasping. Christy Karle was a petite, beautiful blonde.

"Miss Montgomery?" she questioned.

Janet swallowed tightly. Christy's voice was sweet, low and utterly feminine. The hair, the body, the voice—all rolled into one neat package. Odds were, Reese would hire her on the spot.

"You must be Christy Karle," Janet said, fighting to keep the quiver out of her voice. "If you'll follow me, I'll take you to Mr. Edwards' office." She knew she sounded stiff, unfriendly, but until after the shock waned it was unavoidable.

Reese stood as Janet escorted Christy into his office.

"Mr. Edwards, this is Christy Karle," Janet introduced the blonde and noted how Christy moved forward confidently and shook Reese's outstretched hand. Nothing would have induced Janet to check his expression. She was all too aware that his face would be intent with interest, even amusement. To Reese, Christy Karle would be like a dream come true. Without a doubt, Janet realized that Reese was going to hire this woman.

Janet watched as the svelte young woman lowered herself into the chair opposite Reese. Feeling gauche and ugly, Janet awkwardly left the room and closed the door. Determinedly she swallowed the hard lump in her throat and sat at her desk, intending to go about her business. A blonde! Janet wanted to scream with frustration. Instead she buried her face in her hands and took in giant breaths to control the overwhelming force of jealous hostility.

Past experience had taught her she was incapable of handling such deep resentments without God's help. Although Janet was aware that there could never be anything between Reese and herself, she had continued to pray for him daily. Part of her prayers had centered on his relationship with his father. Although it had been extremely painful in the beginning, she had also prayed that Reese would someday discover the true meaning of love the way God intended, with the right woman.

The process of attempting to relinquish her deep feelings for him had begun months before, but to actually see the woman who would take her place in the office, and very likely in his heart, was almost more than she could handle.

Less than ten minutes later Christy Karle stepped out of Reese's office, a brilliant smile lighting up her cobalt blue eyes. "I got the job."

"Congratulations." Janet smiled weakly.

"Everything went so smoothly," Christy breathed out softly. "The employment agency warned me that Mr. Edwards is a stickler for detail, a real bear. They've certainly got him wrong. He's great."

"I think the word's 'wonderful,'" Janet chided mockingly under her breath.

"He didn't test my shorthand skills or give me a typing test. Just a few basic questions."

"I'm pleased everything went so well for you," Janet said without sounding the least bit delighted.

"He said I should start right away."

"Fine." Janet stood, vacating her desk seat. "You sit here so I can explain the computer operating system." Janet wheeled another chair around to her desk. "One thing . . . you aren't allergic to gold, are you?" Janet was thinking of the shining bracelet this girl would probably receive in the next few months. Three months, possibly four, longer if she was smarter.

"No, why?" The blonde head quirked at an inquiring angle.

"No reason."

That afternoon and the next morning proved that if Janet had hand-picked a replacement herself, she couldn't have done better. Christy Karle was perfect, much to Janet's dismay.

Courtesy demanded that Janet invite Christy to lunch with her and Gail.

The petite blonde smiled her appreciation. "I'd like that."

As Janet made the introductions, Gail was giving her roommate sympathetic looks. "This is your replacement?" she asked under her breath as they waited for Christy to freshen up before heading for the small café where they regularly ate lunch.

Janet couldn't do anything more than nod.

"I don't believe it." Gail's hands were clenched at her side, her eyes glinting with anger. "I've heard of some low tricks, but this really takes the cake."

"It's all right." Janet didn't know why she felt like she needed to defend Reese.

"No it isn't," Gail murmured in a low breath. "And not only is it unfair to you, what about Christy? She's like a defenseless lamb walking into the slaughterhouse. Someone should tell her."

"Tell me what?" Christy came out of the rest

room and arched delicately shaped eyebrows in question.

"About the awful food in the cafeteria," Janet said almost desperately. "Be warned."

The look Christy gave her told Janet she wasn't fooled. Her blue eyes narrowed as if she would have liked to ask more. Hurriedly Janet and Gail led the way out the door.

Five minutes after Janet arrived the next morning, Christy walked into the office. She wore a pleated floral dress and her long blonde hair curled away from her face. She was so attractive that for an instant Janet couldn't tear her eyes away from her. The knowledge that Reese wouldn't be able to either brought a throbbing pain to her heart.

Janet had already put on the coffee and together they sorted through the mail.

"I'll take it in," Christy volunteered.

"I usually take in a cup of coffee for Mr. Edwards at the same time. He probably won't notice, so just set it on a bare corner on his desk. If there is one," she added with a half laugh.

Christy took in the coffee and mail as Janet sorted through a list of items her replacement would need to familiarize herself with.

A light bubble of laughter drifted from the room, followed by Reese's chuckle. Janet's eyes rounded with hurt as heated waves of jealousy washed over her. When she had taken in the morning mail, Janet considered herself fortunate to be given a curt nod of acknowledgement.

Friday afternoon, Reese called Janet into his office. "Sit down," he ordered without looking up from the file he was studying.

Janet sat on the edge of the chair, ready to spring upward with the slightest provocation. Suddenly she realized this was probably the last time she would be in this office, or sit in this chair.

"How have things gone with Christy?" he questioned after a couple of minutes, leaning back as he focused his attention on her.

"Very well," she replied primly, resenting the fact Reese and Christy had come to using first names so quickly. "I believe in time Miss Karle will prove to be a valuable asset to Dyna-Flow. She's conscientious, reliable, honest and a hard worker." Only God knew how difficult it was for Janet to praise her replacement.

Reese nodded, his look thoughtful.

Janet stiffened, knowing what was coming. Reese would crisply express his regret at her leaving and offer her best wishes. Janet didn't know if she could bear to listen.

Slowly she stood. "Is that all?"

Reese's look added grimness to the taut features. "No." He also rose, opening the front desk drawer. "I wanted to personally give you this." He handed her a plain business-size envelope.

A frown creasing her brow, Janet accepted the envelope.

"It's your check."

Resentment immediately widened her eyes. "But I've already been paid. The check arrived the first week I left." She swallowed convulsively.

"I thought you would object. That's the reason I decided to personally give it to you. Your coming back to train Christy these past weeks has made as smooth a transition as possible. I want to express my appreciation."

Indignation shot crimson color into her cheeks. "No." She placed the envelope on his desk. "It's not necessary." She drew in a deep breath to steady her nerves. "I appreciate the thought, but I can't accept it."

Reese walked to the other side of the room. Janet's gaze followed him, but she wasn't capable of studying him for long without betraying her love. When he turned around, she quickly glanced away.

He stood with his hands in his pockets as Janet had seen him do a thousand times before. His features were unreadable, but when he spoke to her his voice was filled with some emotion she didn't recognize. "It's such a little thing. I'd like to see your last day here pass without an argument. Won't you take the check, Janet?"

He was right, it was a little thing. And it could be several weeks until she located another job.

Her hands were still clenched in front of her as she decided. Was it any different from the bonus he'd given her at Christmas?

"Janet?" he questioned softly.

Her lips trembled slightly as she met his gaze and gently nodded her head.

His all-male smile seemed to reach across the distance of the room and caress her. Janet basked in the warmth of its glow.

"Thank you," he offered simply.

She took the plain envelope and turned to leave.

"On your way out would you ask Christy to come into my office? I'd like to go over some things with her."

Her hands coiled at her sides, Janet walked out of his office, and out of his life.

Christy gave her a funny look and Janet realized that she probably looked ashen. Two years of her life were over, gone.

"Janet, are you okay?"

She shook her head as if to snap herself out of the self-imposed trance. "Sure." She paused before adding, "Mr. Edwards would like to see you."

Christy automatically reached for her pencil and pad and knocked politely before stepping into the other room. Janet was grateful for these last minutes alone. This room was filled with memories, and she wanted a couple of minutes to privately make her farewells.

Her fingertips ran lightly over the top of the Simplex. A wealth of recent reminiscences came to mind. A smile toyed at her mouth. How silly she had been to allow this machine to frighten her so. The typewriter, her trusted friend, now was stationed in a corner. Janet only used it to type envelopes these days.

Gail arrived a few minutes later and stuck her head in the door. "Are you ready?"

Janet looked up, surprised at the intrusion. "Yes, I think so." She took her coat down and after one final sweeping look at the room turned and left without a backward glance.

Several friends stopped to wish her well on her way to the elevator. By the time they arrived at the parking lot, tears had welled in her eyes.

"Regrets?" Gail glanced at her as they got into the car and turned the ignition key.

"Lots," Janet admitted truthfully. "When I left before, I didn't have time to think about all the friends I was going to miss, or the consequences of my actions. Now that the time has finally come for me to leave, I can't help asking myself if I'm really doing the right thing."

"Are you?" Gail's voice was heavy with concern.

"Yes." The lone word was expelled with a sudden rush of pain. "Yes," she repeated, "I'm sure."

• • •

Joel sat between Janet and her mother during the church service Sunday morning. Restlessly he twisted and turned, crossed, then uncrossed his legs. Loudly he dropped the hymnal. Finally Janet took the book out of his hands.

"What's the matter with you today?" she whispered irritably. "You're acting like you've got ants in your pants."

Joel giggled. "I'm looking for Mr. Reese."

A cold numbness spread over her and she forced herself to smile. "I doubt that he'll be coming back. Now pay attention."

Joel cast her an accusing glare. "No, he's coming. He told me he was coming. If he doesn't, it's your fault."

Her fault. Janet sighed as her brother's words seemed to touch off a swarm of guilty feelings. For years Janet had worried about her Christian witness. She wasn't like her father; she was uncomfortable standing before a group or teaching. She worried that she would never effectively share her faith as she wanted. Shortly after she had made a complete commitment to Christ, her father had explained that not every Christian could be a preacher. But every Christian was a witness. Now she must be satisfied that her faith had been her witness to Reese. Somehow it seemed so inadequate.

As the congregation stood to sing the closing

hymn, Joel stood on the pew and turned around to look out over the people. With a swift jerk, Leonora Montgomery brought him down.

"He's here," he informed Janet with a satisfied smirk. "I told you he would be." Content now, Joel opened the hymnal and began singing loudly.

Reese here? At church? Surely Joel was mistaken. If she was cold and numb before, now she felt like a statue, rooted to one spot. Her father offered the final blessing and ended the service and still Janet stood immobile, unable to turn around.

"Aren't you going to say hello?" Joel chastised, pulling at her coat sleeve.

"Another time," she said in a tortured whisper. She moved out of the pew and down the long aisle in a reflex movement. Purposely she delayed leaving the church as long as possible, making excuses to chat with old friends and acquaintances. When the church was empty, she moved the hymnals to the end of the pews in the back rows. The job was usually done by the ushers after the evening service, but there were seldom enough people to fill the church Sunday evenings.

"Hello, Janet."

Her heart skipped a beat. As if in slow motion, she finished bringing the last red hymnal to the end of the pew before looking up.

"Hello, Reese." She clenched her Bible to her breast with both hands.

"Could we talk a minute?"

"What do you want to talk about?"

"Us." He chuckled. "And before you can say it, yes, there is an *us*."

Janet took a step backward and Reese advanced into the pew. He was so close, she could smell the musk aftershave he wore, so close she could read something in his eyes she had never before witnessed.

The back of her legs were pressing into the hard wooden seat and because it was impossible to go farther, Janet sat down.

Reese moved to sit beside her and reached for her hand. "I find it fitting that we should have this discussion in church," he said, concentrating his eyes on her hands. He hesitated before continuing. "I love you, Janet."

"No." The word was sharp and filled with disbelief. Why was Reese doing this? Did he want to hurt her even more? She yanked her hands free and rushed into the foyer.

Reese followed, stopping her just before she reached the huge double-door entry. "I'm not going to let you run away."

Her face was flushed and it felt like her whole body was trembling. Tears blurred her eyes as she studied the worn rust-colored carpeting.

"Look at me," he demanded, a finger lifting her chin so that their eyes could meet. "I expected some kind of reaction when I said I loved you, but not tears."

"Don't lie to me," she snapped angrily. "How can you say you love me?"

A smile threatened to crack the hard line of his mouth. "If you want the truth, it wasn't that easy. I should have told you how I felt months ago." He paused and pushed a hand through his dark brown hair. "If I hadn't been so blind, I would have recognized what was happening between us."

"How can you claim to love me when you think I'm a hypocrite?"

"A hypocrite?" He hurled the word back at her disbelievingly. "You're the most genuine person I've ever met."

Janet whirled around and started out the door. She wasn't going to listen to his lies, not when she had seen the evidence of his true feelings with her own eyes.

"Janet." He reached the door before she did, blocking her path.

"Don't lie to me, Reese Edwards. I found the caricature. I know exactly what you think of me."

"You saw?" Janet could feel the tension flow out of him. "My love, if you'd only asked me at the time I would have explained why I drew you as I did. I picture you as an angel God has sent into my life to show me His love. Yet at the same time, a devil because you tempt me more than any woman."

"Don't confuse physical desire with love." She

225

remained defensive because it was impossible to believe what he was saying.

"My dear Janet, after the way I've lived my life, believe me, I know the difference. What I feel for you is genuine."

Still unsure and afraid, Janet studied his face, every groove, every line, fearing what she would find. Instead she read confirmation in the shining light of his eyes.

"Oh, Reese," she whispered, and pressed a hand to her forehead. "I've loved you so long."

Instantly she was drawn into his arms as he buried his face in her hair. His arms surrounded her, crushing her close. "I thought I'd lost you," he breathed in deeply. "For a horrible minute I feared it might be too late." Tenderly he kissed the top of her head and relaxed his hold. "Let's sit down, there's so much to explain."

A single pew ran the length of the foyer. With a hand at her waist, Reese led her to the seat.

Leaning forward, elbows on his knees, Reese rubbed his face. "I'm not exactly sure where to begin."

Janet placcd a comforting arm over his back. "It's not necessary, there's no need for you to tell me anything."

The look he gave her told Janet that if they hadn't been in a church he would have reached over and greedily kissed her. "It's necessary, at least it is for me."

Knowingly Janet nodded.

"I once told you I was a model child. I was. As an only child, I felt it was my duty not to worry my parents. I was close to both, eager to please, eager to satisfy. Dad was grooming me to take over the business and I went off to college carefree, my future assured. I'd only been gone a few months when my mother arrived on campus to tell me she and Dad were getting a divorce. I was stunned. As far as I knew, my parents were happily married. Within a year my mother was dead. I'm convinced she died of a broken heart. The problem was they were both so stubborn. Neither of them wanted the divorce, yet neither one was willing to admit fault. After Mom died, Dad changed. The guilt he carried was so heavy I sometimes wondered if he would ever be the same father I'd known. In a matter of months my safe, secure world was shattered. I watched as my classmates married and divorced. Again and again I witnessed the breakdown of the family. Long ago I'd decided loving someone was too painful. I dated and used a certain type of woman because I knew there was never any danger of my falling in love with them. I was too sensible to love a Bunny Jacobs or a Barbara Martin. I realize now how wrong it was to use them that way."

Their hands entwined, Janet sighed and hung her head. "I was terribly jealous of every one of your blondes. When I ordered them flowers or jewelry it was like a part of me died inside."

Reese raised her hand and gently kissed her knuckles. "I'm thirty-four; one would assume that by now I would be smart enough to know the difference between love and sex. I did know I was unhappy. There seemed to be this hole in my life, a void. That was why I bought the cabin. In my own way I was seeking God, seeking an answer to my own restlessness, and an answer to my father's guilt. I firmly believe God sent you into my life for this reason."

"In the beginning the feelings you had for me were only physical, weren't they?" It hurt to ask, but Janet felt she had to know.

"Yes, I admit my invitation for you to spend the night was cheap. I've thought about that several times since and wondered how you've put up with me."

Happiness radiating from her deep blue eyes, Janet met his gaze and smiled. "It's easy when you love someone."

Reese gently lifted a strand of hair away from her face and pressed a kiss to her cheek. "Everything changed after the day you and Joel were with me at Black Hawk. Your faith touched me unlike anything I've known. I've always thought of Christians as goody-goody types who go around issuing meaningless platitudes. Not you, not Joel. When your brother was born you didn't leap in the air and shout praises to God. You struggled and came to terms with his handicap just as I'm sure your parents did in their own way. Meeting Christianity face to face like that shook me. I did the only thing I've known for the past few years. I ran and hid. I don't think I'll ever forget the look on your face when you confronted me that next week—confusion, hurt, pride. I could have kicked myself afterward, but I didn't know what else to do. I've been ready for a long time for your love, Janet. Ready to commit my life to the Lord. Now I'm ready to commit my love to you." He stood and offered her his hand. "I feel that since we're in church God should be our witness."

Hand in hand, they walked up the center aisle of the church and knelt at the altar. Kneeling beside her, Reese brought out a diamond engagement ring from his pocket. "Will you share my life, Janet?"

The lump of wondrous joy blocked her throat, so that all Janet could do was nod.

Gently, Reese lifted her hand and slipped the ring on her finger. Their hands joined and their heads bowed as each offered a prayer of dedication to one another and to God.

When Janet lifted her face tears of happiness had filled her eyes. Ever so gently, Reese folded her into his arms. "I love you. I'll love you all my life."

"And I, you."

Together they stood, arms looped around each other's waist. "I think we should go outside. I know two anxious sets of parents, and one brother, who are waiting for the results."

Janet sighed contentedly and laid her head against his shoulder. "Your father's in on this too?"

"Oh yes, both Dad and I have had this great need in our lives. The first thing your father—"

"My dad?" she questioned in open astonishment.

"Yes, your dad. He sat us both down, told us about the free gift of salvation and the price Christ paid to make us that offer. Later he sent us home to memorize 2 Corinthians 5:17."

"And did you?" Janet asked with an amused grin.

"Therefore if any man be in Christ, he is a new creature: old things are passed away; behold, all things are become new." He said it confidently. "I am a new man, Janet. A new man in Christ, a new man in your love."

Joel was in the parking lot when they walked out of the church. "Did you ask her?" He raced to Reese's side breathlessly.

Without waiting for Reese to respond, Janet held out her finger, the solitary diamond sparkling a rainbow's array of color.

"Didn't I tell you, Janny," Joel declared proudly. "Mr. Reese told me the first Sunday he came to church that he'd be back every Sunday to sit with you because he wanted to marry you."

"That was your secret?" Janet questioned.

"And I didn't tell anybody."

Arms looped around these two men she loved, Janet proceeded to the parsonage, where her parents and future father-in-law were waiting.

Unexpectedly the sun broke through the thick layer of gray clouds and burst forth over the earth, boldly casting its rays on the three as they walked. Janet paused and glanced to the sky, a tear in her eye. It was almost as if God were looking down and shining on them.

Center Point Large Print
600 Brooks Road / PO Box 1
Thorndike ME 04986-0001 USA

(207) 568-3717

US & Canada:
1 800 929-9108
www.centerpointlargeprint.com